HOWL-OWEEN!

Sink your teeth into these:

MY BROTHER THE WEREWOLF

Cry Wolf!

Puppy Love!

Howl-oween!

Tail Spin — *coming soon* . . .

MY SISTER THE VAMPIRE

Switched

Fangtastic!

Revamped!

Vampalicious

Take Two

Love Bites

Lucky Break

Star Style

Twin Spins!

Date with Destiny

Flying Solo

Stake Out!

Double Disaster!

Flipping Out!

Sienna Mercer

MY BROTHER THE WEREWOLF

HOWL-OWEEN!

EGMONT

EGMONT

We bring stories to life

With special thanks to Lisa Fiedler

My Brother the Werewolf: Howl-oween! first published in Great Britain 2013
by Egmont UK Limited
The Yellow Building, 1 Nicholas Road, London W11 4AN

Copyright © Working Partners Ltd 2013
Created by Working Partners Limited, London WC1X 9HH

ISBN 978 1 4052 6797 7

1 3 5 7 9 10 8 6 4 2

A CIP catalogue record for this title is available from the British Library

Typeset by Avon DataSet Ltd, Bidford on Avon, Warwickshire
Printed and bound in Great Britain by the CPI Group

55611/1

EGMONT LUCKY COIN

Our story began over a century ago, when seventeen-year-old
Egmont Harald Petersen found a coin in the street.

He was on his way to buy a flyswatter, a small hand-operated
printing machine that he then set up in his tiny apartment.

The coin brought him such good luck that today Egmont has
offices in over 30 countries around the world. And that lucky
coin is still kept at the company's head offices in Denmark.

To Shannon, Maddie, Sam and Sophia, with love.

Chapter One

Daniel Packer stepped into the bathroom. His identical twin brother, Justin, was already in there, battling a lock of his hair that seemed determined to stick straight up rather than lie flat.

Daniel rolled his eyes. 'Good thing you're from a family of werewolves and not vampires,' he said.

'Yeah?' Justin frowned. 'Why is that?'

'Because if you were a vampire, you'd have no reflection . . . so you wouldn't be able to spend *so* much time admiring yourself in the mirror.'

'Funny,' said Justin. 'First of all, vampires don't exist. And secondly, for your information, it's *important* to look good for a date.'

'If you say so.' Daniel glanced down at the tile floor and added silently, *I wouldn't know.*

'Besides,' grumbled Justin. 'I probably would have missed out on the vampire gene, just like I missed out on the werewolf one.'

Daniel felt a familiar pang of guilt. Up until their birthday a few months ago, he had been completely oblivious to the fact that he was from a mixed human–werewolf family. He was what his dad had jokingly called an 'unaware-wolf'.

Since the day they were born, their Lupine father had known that one of them would transform on their thirteenth birthday. From the time the boys were old enough to walk, it was Justin who had shown the signs of being a wolf: speed, strength, an interest in sports. So, while their dad had let Justin in on the family secret at a young age, Daniel was kept in the dark. Then, to everyone's shock (mostly Daniel's!) it had not been the super-jock twin who had turned into a howling hairy beast, but the sensitive songwriter.

Right now, though, it seemed to Daniel that *Justin* was the one undergoing the major metamorphosis. Of course, Daniel could explain Justin's new obsession with his appearance in two words:

Riley Carter.

Since Justin and the blonde over-achiever had officially become an 'item', Justin's bathroom prep time had practically quadrupled.

'What exactly are you trying to accomplish?' Daniel asked, motioning towards the shaggy layers of his brother's latest hairstyle.

'I don't know,' said Justin, patting down the rebellious lock with such force Daniel worried his twin might give himself a concussion. 'I guess I'm shooting for the *I don't care how I look* look.'

'Then . . . how about . . . *not* caring how you look?' Daniel suggested with a chuckle.

'You don't get it,' sighed Justin. 'I can't not care. I really want to impress Riley tonight.'

'She's already impressed. I mean, she agreed to be your girlfriend,' Daniel reasoned. *I just wish I could say the same for Debi*, he thought.

Justin fiddled with the collar of his shirt. 'Yeah, but I can't take anything for granted,' he muttered.

Overnight, it seemed, Daniel's twin had gone from simply running a towel over his hair after a shower to actually attempting to 'style' it. This even involved borrowing a can of something called 'Volumising Mousse' from their mother's dressing table. And the wardrobe! Justin was suddenly throwing around words like 'trendy', 'hip' and even 'stylish ensemble'. Before, the only thing that mattered to him about his clothes was whether or not they were clean (and sometimes not even that), but now he wanted to know if certain shirts 'went better' with jeans or with khakis, and which of his belts made the best 'fashion statement'. Daniel had always thought that keeping your trousers from falling down was really the only statement that mattered, but clearly Justin had other ideas.

Now, here they were, on the verge of being late for the Pine Wood Fall Fair, and Justin was still trying to flatten the unruly lock of hair.

'We should get going before the girls leave without us,' Daniel prompted.

Finally, Justin turned away from the mirror. 'I'm ready,' he announced, then frowned. 'But what about you?'

'I'm ready.'

Justin raised one eyebrow and took in Daniel's outfit – a gray zip hoodie hanging open over a vintage Rolling Stones T-shirt and faded jeans. When his gaze fell on his brother's shoes his eyes flew open. 'What's with the mismatched kicks, Bro?'

Daniel wriggled his feet inside the one black Converse high top sneaker and the one battered combat boot and felt suddenly defensive. 'Just something I'm trying out,' he fibbed. The truth was, he'd intended to wear two Converse sneakers, but he'd had a slight *accident* when putting them on. He was so nervous about the evening ahead that his wolf claws had sprouted without warning, and before he knew what was happening, his right Converse high top had been torn in half. And since he would never have found his left combat boot without trashing his room in a full-scale search, he'd decided to save

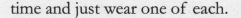

time and just wear one of each.

At the time, it had seemed kind of creative and rock 'n' roll-ish.

Now though, he wondered if it just looked stupid.

Still, he was in a hurry to get going, so he shrugged and gave his brother a grin. 'Think of it as *my* fashion statement,' he said.

Justin rolled his eyes.

'Well, it's not like I'm going on an actual date,' said Daniel, hoping he didn't sound as sulky as he felt. 'You and Riley are a couple. Debi and I are . . .'

'You're what?' Justin prompted.

Good question, Daniel thought.

He was pretty crazy about the new girl across the street, with the dazzling red hair and the cute smile. And they had been spending lots of time together. He thought, or at least he *hoped*, she liked him the same way he liked her. But he certainly didn't have the guts to ask her. And for some reason, it just seemed too risky to let her know how he felt. What if she didn't *like*-like him, the way he *like*-liked her? What if she laughed at him?

He had enough to deal with already, what with his whole changing-into-a-werewolf problem. If having a girlfriend caused the kind of craziness he was seeing on Justin, Daniel just wasn't sure he'd be able to handle it.

He stifled the wolf-like growl of frustration threatening to rumble up from his throat and answered his brother's question: 'Just friends, that's what we are.'

'If you say so,' said Justin, rolling his eyes and giving his hair one more pat.

Daniel grabbed Justin's arm, tugged him out of the bathroom and downstairs to where their parents waited in the front hall.

'Have fun at the Fall Fair, boys,' Dad called.

'Don't eat too many candy apples,' Mom added. Then she gave Daniel a kiss on the cheek, and reached out to smooth down the one spiky lock of Justin's hair.

'Don't touch the 'do!' he said, and was about to sprint back up to the bathroom, but Daniel grabbed him by the arm again and dragged him towards the front door.

'Want to impress your new girlfriend?' he said, grabbing their jackets and giving his brother a friendly nudge out the door. 'Try punctuality.'

As they made their way across the street to Debi's house, Daniel was surprised that there was not a single Halloween decoration to be seen. Every house on their block had at least a pumpkin on the porch, which made Debi's house look strangely out of place.

And speaking of strange . . . Daniel's chest

was suddenly feeling . . . well, strange. These days, he was getting used to the itchy skin, the tingling teeth, the sprouting claws that signified the switch from human to wolf. For one panicked moment, he was afraid that was exactly what was happening now.

But when he ran his tongue across his front teeth and didn't feel any fangs growing, he knew this tightening in his chest and burning tingle in the pit of his stomach was something else. *This* feeling was an entirely human sensation . . . jealousy.

Daniel had never been jealous of Justin before. The twins were completely different, in everything but their identical looks, so they'd never had cause to feel competitive with one another. Daniel was truly happy that his brother had finally got together with Riley – he just couldn't help wishing that he, too, had a girlfriend of his own. Namely, Debi.

Even if it did mean a few extra minutes – OK, *hours* – in front of the mirror and a total wardrobe upgrade, he wanted to be dating her for real. He wished tonight wasn't some silly 'just friends' outing, tagging along after the eighth grade mega-couple 'Riley and Justin'. Daniel figured any day now, their classmates would be calling them something goofy like *'Rustin'* or *'Jiley'*.

Suddenly the word *'Danbi'* flew into his mind. He immediately felt silly.

They climbed the steps to Debi's front door. The house was fairly big, with a garage to one side of the door. Newly planted flowers were settling in under the window to the other side. It was a nice, homely home – much more welcoming than when Mackenzie Barton used to live here – but Daniel seemed to be suddenly frozen in place.

'Apparently,' said Justin, 'if one of us presses that black button there –' he pointed at the doorbell – 'it makes a sound that lets the people inside know we're out here waiting.'

'Yeah.' Daniel gulped, unable to bring himself to press the button, or think of a witty comeback to his brother's teasing.

'Guess it's gonna be me then,' said Justin with a shrug. Then, clearly enjoying torturing his brother, he moved his finger towards the bell in super-*super* slow-motion, as though his arm was moving through thick toffee.

Don't turn, don't turn, don't turn, Daniel chanted in his head, although he wasn't sure if he was telling himself not to turn into a werewolf, or not to turn and run away from Debi's house!

I should be way past the whole panicky thing, he thought to himself. *Maybe I'd better just forget about asking Debi to be my girlfriend altogether. If the idea of ringing her doorbell paralyses me this bad, asking her out for real would probably put me in a coma!*

When Mr Morgan – Debi's dad – opened the front door he smiled broadly. 'Well, hello there!' he bellowed in his friendly way. He was wearing a bulky sweater and holding a newspaper and looked like a father from an old-time TV ad; behind him, Daniel could see that there was a roaring fire in the hearth. Unfortunately, his musky scented shaving lotion was so strong, it was making Daniel's wolf nose twitch, and his eyes water.

'Hey, Mr Morgan,' said Justin, accepting the handshake Debi's father offered.

Daniel couldn't seem to get his voice to work up the volume to even say hello. When *he* shook Mr Morgan's hand, he was so afraid his wolf strength might kick in that he barely even closed his fingers. This resulted in him giving the world's wimpiest handshake.

Way to impress a girl's dad, Daniel.

'Hey, guys,' came a voice down the hall.

Daniel peered around Mr Morgan to see Debi emerging from the living room and approaching the front door. She was smiling her prettiest smile and her hair – which was the same colour as the flames dancing in the fireplace behind her – was pulled into a low side-ponytail, with a few stray curls bobbing around her temples.

And talk about a 'stylish ensemble'. Clearly, Debi hadn't had any problems when it came to putting together an outfit for the Fall Fair. She was wearing a denim shirt under a burnt-orange v-neck sweater that looked impossibly soft. The sweater was tunic-length, coming down over her brown leggings. She wore tall caramel-coloured leather boots, and a puffy vest jacket that was the exact same shade as dark chocolate.

She looked . . . kind of perfect.

Not overdressed, but totally put together –

the way a girl might dress for . . . *a date?* Daniel felt a flutter of joy thinking that Debi had gone to the trouble of looking terrific for him. Then the happy flutter turned to a knot of doubt; it was entirely possible that she was simply dressing nicely because this would be her first ever Pine Wood Fall Fair, and she didn't want to look shabby.

So maybe this *wasn't* a date? Daniel had no way of knowing.

What he *did* know was that, compared to Debi's gorgeously coordinated outfit, his own mis-matched shoes now seemed completely ridiculous.

Daniel felt his eyes beginning to sting and feared he may go furball, until he realised it was just Mr Morgan's aftershave attacking him again.

Debi was looking at his shoes.

OK, so now she thinks I'm the weirdest weirdo in the whole weird world!

15

She quickly snapped her eyes upwards and blinked at Daniel. She didn't ask about the combat boot/sneaker combo, which was a relief, but when she gave Justin a smile and told him she really liked his shirt, Daniel almost turned and bolted.

Mr Morgan gave Debi a kiss on the forehead. 'OK, kids. You have fun!'

Fun? Daniel wondered if that was even possible.

As they made their way around the corner to Riley's house, Justin asked Debi about the lack of decorations. 'Are you guys anti-Halloween or something?' he joked. After all, he wasn't tongue-tied by a crush. 'Or maybe allergic to pumpkins?'

Debi laughed, and Daniel wished he'd been the one to ask the question. But his mind was too busy freaking out about his stupid shoes to start a conversation.

'It may seem that way now,' Debi explained, 'but tomorrow will be a whole different story. 'I'm surprised you couldn't see from the doorway. My dad has a whole giant blueprint of his "decorations scheme" laid out on the coffee table. Drawn to scale and everything. Strobe lights, fake gravestones, life-sized monster dummies. He's got "themes" and "motifs" and "narratives" planned. I think he even has the phone number of the local pumpkin farm on his speed dial.'

'That sounds pretty cool,' said Justin.

'Yeah,' Daniel piped up in a croak. 'Cool.'

'You say cool, I say totally embarrassing.' Debi sighed. 'So tell me about the Fall Fair. We used to have a Pumpkin Festival back in Franklin Grove, but it was more for the little kids. You know, face painting and ring toss games and stuff.'

'We've got those,' said Justin. 'But we've also got a lot of more challenging games, too. There's

live entertainment and awesome carnival rides.
Everyone in town shows up and –'

'One time, I won a goldfish!' Daniel blurted
loudly.

Debi looked at him. 'You what?'

Daniel could feel the hair sprouting on the
back of his hands; he quickly shoved them into
his pockets. *Breathe* . . . 'Um, at the fair. When
we were, like, six or seven. I threw a ping-pong
ball into a fish bowl. Won a goldfish. I called
him Basil.'

'Oh.' Debi gave him a sweet smile. Then, to
Daniel's surprise, she placed her hand on the arm
of his sweatshirt. 'That's great.'

Daniel gulped. Physical contact *had* to mean
something, right? Even if it did only last a
fraction of a second.

Daniel was still thinking about it as they
arrived at Riley's house, where they found Mr

Carter raking leaves in the front yard.

'Hiya, kids,' he called, dragging a rake-full of crunchy brown and yellow leaves towards the enormous pile in the middle of the grass.

'Hi, Mr Carter,' said Debi. 'Is Riley ready to go?'

Mr Carter leaned the rake against a tree and brushed his hands against his jeans. 'Let's go inside and find out.'

As they headed for the front porch, Mr Carter chuckled. 'Hey, Daniel. Remember when you were just a little guy and you used to come over here and beg me to let you jump in the leaf piles?'

'Um . . . yeah.' Daniel suddenly felt a little sick; he knew where this was going . . .

'You just loved jumping in those piles. Problem was, after about the third or fourth jump, you'd get a leaf up your sweater and run home crying with your nose running all over the place like a broken tap! Remember?'

Daniel forced himself to nod, and did his best to smile – but his cheeks burned, and it had nothing to do with transforming. This was good, old-fashioned embarrassment.

But Debi was giggling. 'That's so cute!' For the *second time*, she put her hand on Daniel's arm. 'I can just picture you rolling around in the leaves like a puppy. I bet it was adorable.'

Daniel relaxed just a little. She just called him 'adorable'. Maybe it wasn't a total disaster.

When they reached the front porch, Mr Carter opened the front door and called for Riley.

'What is it, Dad?' came her voice from upstairs.

'Your friends are here!' he announced. Then he turned back to grin at Daniel, Debi and Justin. 'I must say, you four are going to be the cutest couple of couples at the fair.'

Daniel wondered what he'd done to Mr Carter to make the man so determined to ruin his life.

Couples?! Of course, deep down he knew Debi's father wasn't trying to humiliate him. He was just being a normal goofy dad. Unfortunately, his idea of small talk was making Daniel's teeth tingle.

'This isn't a double date,' Daniel corrected quickly. 'Not exactly. It's more like a bunch of friends just hanging out together. You know? Buddies, pals. Nothing . . . you know . . . *couple-y* about it.'

'Chill out, Bro,' said Justin. 'You're totally sending the wrong message here!'

Daniel shot his brother a look, then realised that Justin's lips were barely moving; he'd whispered his warning so that only Daniel's super-sensitive wolf ears would register it.

Daniel gave himself a mental face-palm. Everything he had just blurted made it sound as though he hated the idea of being a couple . . . which of course he didn't. Not at all! But for some reason, he didn't want Mr Carter to know that. Why? Maybe because he didn't know how Debi felt about the whole couple issue. The last thing he wanted was to seem like he'd gone all 'moony' if she hadn't.

Then Riley came skipping down the stairs. Out of the corner of his eye, Daniel saw Justin's hand go to his hair.

'Hi, guys!' said Riley. As she reached up to take her jacket from the coat rack, she got her wrist tangled in a scarf. 'Oops,' she said as she gave the scarf a tug, causing an avalanche of ski-hats, woollen coats and windbreakers to spill down from the rack. The clothes landed in a colorful heap on the hall floor.

Another glance at Justin's moony grin told Daniel that his twin found Riley's clumsiness more cute than quirky.

'Sorry,' said Riley, with a frown.

'I'll take care of this,' Mr Carter said, ushering his daughter on to the porch.

'I'm so excited to go to the fair!' Riley gushed, struggling to slip her arm into her bright red pea coat. Unfortunately, this action caused her to miss the first stair and she started to fall! Daniel and Debi gasped as Riley's feet went out from under her. She tumbled forwards, arms flailing, heading for a collision with the brick walkway.

But Justin reacted with a quick leap to place himself in her path, opening his arms to catch her just in time.

It was an amazing save, even for a talented jock like Justin, who was now holding Riley in his arms as though she were as light as a feather . . . a very *clumsy* feather.

Clearly, from the way Riley was looking up at Justin with adoring eyes, she was impressed, too. And as she gave a grateful smile, Daniel's wolf ears could actually hear his brother's heart beating double time.

Debi looked at Riley and Justin with a dreamy smile. 'The knight in shining armour rescues his damsel in distress,' she whispered.

'Yeah,' grumbled Daniel. 'He's a regular superhero.'

He wished Debi knew that he would totally catch *her* if she ever took such a scary fall. In fact, for one crazy moment he considered sticking out his foot and tripping her, just to prove it. But something told him that, save or no save, a boy did *not* try to trip up the girl he wanted to be his girlfriend. Even Daniel knew that was a majorly bad idea.

Instead, the only thing Debi knew was that he had told Mr Carter that they were *not* a couple on a date. He felt that knot in his stomach again as he watched Justin gallantly help his girlfriend on with her coat.

'Thanks, Justin,' Riley whispered, sweeping a lock of golden hair out of her big brown eyes.

Then the couple and the non-couple headed off towards the fair.

As they walked, Daniel continued to sulk about having no way to prove his own heroism to Debi. But when they turned the next bend, he spotted something ahead with his wolf vision: a pumpkin that had been smashed on the sidewalk. When Daniel saw the broken pieces with the gooey guts spilling out, inspiration struck.

Debi was so involved with admiring Riley's coat she didn't notice the slippery mess of pumpkin slime and seeds in her path.

When she was two steps away from the goop, Daniel cried, 'Look out!' then immediately flung himself between Debi and the smashed pumpkin.

Unfortunately, he underestimated his wolf momentum, and instead of simply blocking her from stepping in the mess, he lost his balance and went sailing face first into the puddle of slime.

The next thing he knew, he was wiping orange goop from his eyes and spitting out pumpkin seeds.

'Oh, no!' cried Debi. 'Daniel, what happened?'

Daniel pulled a rotting chunk of pumpkin shell out of his hair and sighed. 'I slipped,' he muttered.

'Are you OK?'

Just humiliated beyond belief, he wanted to say. What he actually said was, 'Yeah. I'm fine.' Then he used his sleeve to wipe the slime off his cheek.

Chapter Two

Catching Riley in his arms had been a lot easier than some of the catches Justin had to make in football practice. But even though rescuing his girlfriend from a painful fall hadn't been that hard, or taken place in front of hundreds of cheering fans, Justin couldn't help thinking it was more satisfying. *I could get used to this heroic boyfriend role*, he thought to himself as the group arrived at their destination.

The fairground was teeming with people. It seemed as if the whole town had turned out. And Justin was pleased to see that every kid and teacher from Pine Wood Junior High made it a point to smile at the couple of couples . . . or, the couple and whatever Daniel and Debi actually were.

'*Rustin/Jiley*' – arriving at the Fall Fair on their first *official* date as an *official* couple.

It was awesome . . . and a little bit terrifying. All he had to do was make it *official*: and that meant holding her hand.

OK, well, maybe he didn't *have* to. But he sure did want to.

This was something he'd been thinking about for a while now. He'd seen some of the older couples from school holding hands in the bus lines, and even in the corridors. But at school, Riley's hands tended to be filled with clipboards and notebooks and agendas . . . most of which she'd eventually drop all over the floor. Here at the Fall Fair her hands were completely free.

Totally and completely holdable.

Justin took a deep breath and casually let his left hand brush against her right. He let it linger there for a moment as they made their way through the crowd. Kids were dashing back and forth, and some of the seventh grade boys were trying to cut in line for the Spider Coaster, which had a reputation for being the scariest ride at the fair.

Not scarier than trying to hold your girlfriend's hand for the very first time, he thought.

Taking a deep breath, he flexed his fingers and reached out towards Riley's hand.

Closer . . .

Closer . . .

'Hello there, Riley!'

Startled, Justin jerked his hand back as though he'd touched hot coals. He turned to see Riley's Social Studies teacher waving at them.

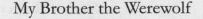

'Hi, Mrs Chase!' cried Riley.

'I hate to bother you while you're enjoying the fair with this nice young man,' said Mrs Chase, 'but I just wanted to tell you that I received approval from the school board about the fund-raiser you proposed to buy books for that orphanage in Zimbabwe.'

'Really?' Riley beamed. 'That's awesome!'

Does Riley ever slow down? Justin wondered. For all he knew, she was planning not only to purchase the books but to hop on a plane and deliver them to the Zimbabwean kids in person.

'Let's meet during study hall on Monday,' Mrs Chase said, then hurried off towards the dunking booth.

As Riley began walking again, Justin's mind quickly shifted back to his mission. He carefully swung his arm so that his knuckles continued to gently bump against hers. It was like a warm-up lap before the real, actual hand-holding.

He told himself not to be so wimpy. They were 'boyfriend-and-girlfriend' now. In a relationship. An item. Holding hands was a perfectly natural next step.

So why am I so nervous?

They paused at a booth selling big pink clouds of candyfloss in paper cones.

'Want one?' he asked, his voice a little scratchy.

'No thanks,' said Riley. 'I'm saving my appetite for the fresh donut booth. It's such an autumn-ish treat, don't you think?'

'Absolutely,' said Justin.

She smiled and his knees almost buckled.

As they fell into step again, Justin glanced around for Daniel and Debi; he caught a glimpse of them through the crowd. They had wandered over to admire the handmade quilt display (well, *Debi* was admiring – Daniel was standing there looking slightly pained). Justin decided there was no point in waiting, his brother and his non-date would catch up eventually. Besides, hand-holding was challenging enough *without* an audience.

And this was the moment. He was going to do it. Now!

He took a deep breath, spread his fingers wide, then gently closed them around Riley's.

Success!

To his great relief, she didn't jump in surprise, or pull away or turn and scream furiously in his face,'*What do you think you're doing, Justin Packer?!*'

She did do *something*, though . . . she gave his palm a quick squeeze.

As they continued walking, Justin began to feel prickles of panic. Was he employing the *proper* hand-holding technique? As with everything else about dating, he was sure there was a right way and a wrong way to hold hands with a girl, like there was only one way to arrange your fingers on the laces of a football when trying to throw a perfect pass. But how was he to know what it was? His fingers seemed perfectly intertwined with hers, but his wrist was bent at an awkward angle. He'd gone over when he probably should have gone under, which was making things slightly uncomfortable.

He felt a wave of embarrassment for being such a romance rookie, but Riley either didn't notice or didn't want to insult him by correcting his form. What mattered was, she didn't let go, and this made Justin feel terrific. They could work the bugs out later, he figured. He didn't mind the idea of practising at all. And maybe that was part of the whole relationship deal – figuring things out . . . together.

Suddenly, it felt as if they'd been holding hands every day of their lives.

'How about those donuts?' he said, without even the slightest catch in his voice.

'I'd love some,' said Riley.

But as they headed off in the direction of the donut booth, Justin discovered that walking while holding hands was not as easy as the older kids made it look.

They had to keep dodging people as they went, and Riley's lack of coordination was *not* helping. She zigged when he zagged; she veered left when he leaned right.

Just when the donut booth was in sight, Justin spotted an enthusiastic toddler running towards them.

Uh-oh . . . What do I do? He wondered about letting go, then thought that he'd better not – it had taken him too long to hold on to her hand in the first place!

Justin's heart sped up as the little boy

34

scampered closer. If he didn't do something soon, the tot would collide with their clasped hands at full speed.

He instinctively lifted his hand in the air like a human drawbridge, but since Riley didn't understand his intention, she wound up spinning under his arm like a ballroom dancer.

'Justin, what are you –?' Riley managed to gasp, but just at the halfway point in her dance turn, her knees crossed, her ankle twisted and she wobbled. Justin used his free arm to reach around behind her and hold her upright.

He let out a huge sigh of relief. Not only had the toddler escaped unharmed, but he'd managed to keep Riley on her feet for the second time that day. He grinned at Riley, who gave him a grateful smile in return.

He'd never realised dating would be such a contact sport.

35

As they followed the smell of donuts, Justin was so mesmerised by the feeling of Riley's hand wrapped up in his he didn't notice that Daniel and Debi had caught up to them and were now walking only a few steps behind.

He also didn't see Kyle Hunter, the Pine Wood Junior High football captain and some other players approaching until the last moment.

'Packers in stereo,' Kyle joked.

His fellow '*Beasts*' – always at his side – laughed as though he had told the first joke they'd ever heard.

Kyle met Justin's eyes and grinned. 'Hey, *Justin*,' he said pointedly, then glanced beyond Justin to look closely at the other twin, 'and *Daniel*.'

'Wow.' Riley giggled. 'I guess I'm not the only one who can tell these two apart.'

'Well, it's not easy,' said Kyle, his eyes darting back and forth between the twins. 'But it was pretty obvious that this was Justin since he's the one holding your hand.'

Justin willed himself not to blush as the Beasts broke into a teasing chorus of '*ooooohhhhs*', and wolf whistles – well, most of the Beasts. At the back of the group, Ed Yancey and Caleb Devlin had broken into an impromptu game of 'Mercy'. They were laughing while they wrestled each other, but Justin couldn't help cringing as they moved closer to one of the stands – with their super wolf-strength, they could make a real mess if they crashed into it. He looked at Daniel, and could tell that his brother was doing the same.

'I guess that makes sense,' Riley said to Kyle.

'Sure it does,' said Kyle. 'I mean, unless they decided to play some kind of a joke and switch places. You know, one twin pretending to be the other . . . for *some* reason.'

Justin willed himself not to look at Daniel, for

fear that their expressions would give them away.

Had Kyle somehow guessed their secret?

'That would be pretty silly,' said Debi. 'Justin and Daniel may *look* alike, but underneath, they're actually quite different.'

Kyle grinned, and lowered one eyebrow at Justin. 'Ain't that the truth,' he said.

'Hey, c'mon,' Caleb piped up, disentangling himself from Ed. 'Let's ride the Tilt-a-Whirl. I want to see if it makes Chris cry again, like it did last year.' With that, the Beasts moved off, laughing and throwing fake punches at each other.

Justin knew that even a phony punch from one of those guys could knock a regular kid halfway across the fairground. Even when they weren't in wolf mode, they were a powerfully strong bunch.

He also knew that Kyle was up to something. The way he'd been so careful to call each twin by name, and that remark about one pretending to be the other.

Has he guessed I'm not a werewolf like him?

Justin was jolted out of his thoughts by a firm tug from Riley, who was still holding his hand. 'Donuts and hot apple!' she cried, pointing at the booth just up ahead. 'Doesn't that sound delicious?'

Smiling at the prospect of treating his girlfriend to this perfect autumn snack, Justin nodded. *I can worry about the Kyle and the Beasts later,* he thought to himself. *Right now, I want to make the most of my first ever date.* The next thing he knew, he was following Riley to the donut stand. The smells of warm, sugary dough and apple juice filled the air.

'Two donuts and two hot apples, please,' Riley said to the man in the white apron.

'That'll be four dollars,' the man replied,

ladling the steaming drink into two paper cups. 'Fifty cents extra for a cinnamon stick.'

Uh-oh. Justin suddenly realised that his money was in his left front pocket, but his left hand was currently interlocked with Riley's right.

'I'll take a cinnamon stick,' said Riley, before giving Justin a teasing nudge. 'But *he's* not a fan.'

'How did you know I don't like cinnamon?' Justin asked.

'Don't you remember that time in second grade when they served rice pudding in the school cafeteria?' she asked.

Justin didn't, but he said, 'Yeah.'

'Well, I was standing behind you in the lunch line that day, and the lunch lady asked you if you wanted cinnamon sprinkled on your cup of rice pudding. And you said, "No thank you – I don't like cinnamon."'

She was right, of course. Cinnamon made

40

Justin gag. But the fact that she remembered such a tiny detail about him after so many years sent a rush of warmth through him. She actually *knew* things about him. Just like *he* knew that she loved to put peanut butter on Oreo cookies, and that she was allergic to hamsters.

Talk about 'World's Most Perfect Couple'.

Unfortunately, the female half of the World's Most Perfect Couple was using her free hand to reach into her pocket and fish out a handful of dollar bills.

No! Wait! I want to be the gentleman.

But paying for the stuff would either mean letting go of her hand (which he *really* didn't want to do), or reaching around into his left-hand pocket with his right hand to get his money. And unless he was some kind of contortionist, that would be next to impossible.

Before he could think of a way around this

problem, Riley had already handed the donut man the money.

'Uh, thanks . . .' said Justin, wondering what the word for 'opposite of gentleman' was.

For a moment, they just stared at each other. If they were going to carry the drinks *and* the donuts, they were going to need all their hands, and they both knew it.

Reluctantly, Riley released his hand. Justin figured it was probably a good thing since the whole paying debacle had caused his palm to begin to sweat. The last thing he wanted was for Riley to think he had a perspiration problem.

'The games and the rides are *all* on me,' he blurted, taking the paper cup and the donut from the counter. 'In fact, from here on in, the whole day is my treat. OK?'

Riley replied with a wink and a thumbs-up. 'It's a deal.' Then, in true Riley fashion, she took a sip of her drink, burned her lip and dropped her donut.

Justin quickly reached into his pocket, pulled out a dollar and bought her another one. This made him feel so terrific, he felt like he could kiss her.

Start walking, he told himself. *Before you do something impulsive.*

'What ride would you like to go on first?' Riley asked, hurrying to keep up with him, hot apple tipping out of her paper cup.

'Um . . .' Justin wasn't sure; he was still busy trying not to think about what it would be like to kiss her. *Focus, Packer, focus*, he told himself. If he picked a ride that was too scary, she might be upset. If he picked one that was too mild, she might think he was a big chicken. So instead of an answer, he gave her a shrug. 'Whichever,' he said lamely.

'Oh.' Riley's pink-glossed lips turned down in a slight frown. 'Well, would you rather start with the games?'

Another tricky one: he could pick a game he excelled at, like throwing a basketball through a hoop and winning her a giant stuffed octopus, or a lava lamp, or a Pine Wood Fall Fair commemorative coffee mug – but then she might think he was showing off. Of course, if he picked a different game and he lost, he'd be totally embarrassed.

'Well, uh . . .' He shrugged again. 'Up to you,' he mumbled. *Pathetic!*

'OK.' She put a finger to her chin, thinking for a moment. 'Let's start with the rides, before the lines get too long.'

Justin nodded in agreement, but inside he still felt like the most useless boy on the planet. Would Riley eventually get tired of having to make every single decision by herself? He had really thought things would be a lot easier now that they were a couple, but in a lot of ways he was still as confused as he'd been before.

By now, they'd finished their donuts and hot apple juice and had paused to drop their empty cups into a trash can, freeing them up to walk hand in hand once more.

Here we go again! Guts, Packer. You can do this . . .

But to Justin's surprise it was Riley reached out and took *his* hand this time. And she made it seem so easy, getting their fingers adjusted on the first try, without leaving either of their wrists at awkward, uncomfortable angles.

Riley took my *hand!* The gesture made him feel like the luckiest guy in Pine Wood. He wished the Beasts had been around to see that.

As they walked, Riley asked him: 'I was wondering if you'd do me a favour.'

45

'Anything,' Justin answered, much too quickly.

Riley giggled. 'Well, I signed up to do this community service project called Spooky Chaperone on Halloween night. Basically, I just take some little kids out trick-or-treating.'

'Sounds fun,' said Justin. 'But what's the favour?'

'I'd like you to come with me,' she said, a sudden shyness in her voice. 'I mean, that is, if you don't already have other plans for Halloween night.'

If he had, he'd have broken them to be with Riley for sure. But he hadn't. 'I'm free,' he said, with a giant smile. 'So, yeah, I'll definitely be a Scary Bodyguard with you.'

'That's Spooky Chaperone,' she corrected, giggling again. 'And thanks. It'll be fun.'

Ahead of them, the bigger rides loomed against a grey October sky. They could hear children screaming and laughing as they swooped and spun and spiralled through space.

'Think you can handle the terror of the Spider Coaster?' Justin asked.

'I can if I have you with me,' Riley replied sweetly.

Together, they headed for the ride.

Daniel watched in amazement as Justin and Riley went off, hand-in-hand, in the direction of the Spider Coaster. Was it possible that his twin had actually forgotten that Daniel was there?

It certainly seemed that way.

Maybe that's what happened when you held a girl's hand. Maybe it did something to your brain that caused you to forget *everything else in the world.* Or, at least, everything at the fair.

Unfortunately, Daniel was beginning to fear that he'd never find out for himself. They'd been at the fair for a half hour already and he was still no closer to understanding his current situation with Debi.

He was happy that Justin and Riley were having such a terrific time, but their absence was putting an awful lot of pressure on him to be charming and entertaining.

And to make matters worse . . .

Mackenzie Barton was heading their way! And she was staring at Daniel's shoes with a look of undisguised distaste. Daniel prepared himself for one of her trademark snarky comments. But instead –

'OMG! Debi!'

The next thing Daniel knew, the Pine Wood High Head Cheerleader and self-crowned Queen of Mean was throwing her arms around Debi, and squealing as though they hadn't seen each other in decades.

This had Debi and Daniel exchanging confused looks over Mackenzie's shoulder. She had never been very nice to Debi before, so what was up with the bear hug?

'I can't believe you're here!' she cried. 'Why didn't you try and find us the minute you arrived? The whole squad just went on the Ferris wheel together, and now we're going to bob for apples.' Suddenly, Mackenzie gasped in horror; then just as suddenly sighed with relief. 'Oh, right . . . I thought I wasn't wearing my waterproof lip gloss – but I *so* am, so it'll be totally fine.' She took hold of Debi's wrist and began to pull her away. 'C'mon, let's go find the others.'

'Thanks,' said Debi, digging in her heels against Mackenzie's tugging. 'But I'm on a . . .' She paused, her eyes darting quickly towards Daniel.

On a WHAT? A secret mission? A diet? A DATE?

Daniel held his breath, waiting for her to finish her sentence.

Debi cleared her throat. 'Um . . . I mean . . . I'm here with Daniel and Justin and Riley.'

Mackenzie turned to where Justin and Riley were just taking their place in the Spider Coaster line. Her eyebrows were raised, her lips pursed. It was an expression that clearly meant, 'It doesn't *look* that way.'

'So I guess we'll see you around,' said Debi sweetly. 'If that's OK.'

Daniel was shocked at the unexpected feeling of Debi's hand on his sleeve. She was taking his arm! It wasn't quite as cozy as full-on hand-holding, but it definitely didn't suck! He tried not to let the fact that she was probably only doing it to get away from Mackenzie Barton take the shine off his happiness. Debi was reaching out for him, and that was a very good thing.

50

It was one of the *best* things.

'In fact,' Debi was saying, 'Daniel and I were just heading towards the first aid centre. He's not feeling all that well.'

I'm not? 'Right . . . I'm not.' He immediately placed his hands on his stomach and began to groan.

Mackenzie narrowed her eyes. 'What's wrong with him?'

'Not sure,' said Debi quickly. 'It's either the four hot dogs, three bags of popcorn and two chocolate donuts he ate . . .' she grinned, '. . . or he's coming down with some horribly painful and contagious stomach flu.'

Mackenzie's eyes went wide as she took a giant step back.

'But I only had *one* chocolate donut,' Daniel said innocently. Then he pretended to gag.

Mackenzie scurried back another step.

'When did it start?' she demanded.

'Ummmm . . .' Debi said, a thoughtful expression on her face. 'I think it was right *after* we bobbed for apples.'

Mackenzie gulped. 'OK, well, see you later!' She turned on her heel and took off at a sprint, calling out to her cheer squad as she ran. 'Girls! Stop! Step away from the apple basin! We will not be sticking our faces in that flu-infested water!'

When she was gone Debi and Daniel burst into laughter.

'What was *that* about?' asked Daniel. 'I didn't know you two were such good friends.'

'Me neither,' said Debi. 'Maybe she wants to get in good with *me* because she wants to get in good with *Riley*.'

'Why would she want to get in good with Riley?'

'Riley is Homecoming Queen. She's on the popularity fast track.'

'OK,' said Daniel, frowning. 'But why was Mackenzie hugging *you*?'

'Because I'm Riley's best friend. Hugging Riley would look way too much like sucking up. But hugging me is a suck-up once removed.'

Daniel was lost. 'That's really . . .'

'Complicated?'

He nodded. 'Well, your contagious flu bluff was genius,' he said. 'If I'd known that was all it took to send Mackenzie running for the hills, I'd have pretended to be sick my whole childhood.'

'Well, Mackenzie might seem like she has a fear of illnesses, but she has a much bigger phobia than that: an extreme case of FOMO.' When Daniel cocked a quizzical eyebrow Debi giggled. 'It stands for Fear Of Missing Out,' she explained.

Daniel laughed. 'That's brilliant,' he said, truly

impressed. He also liked the fact that Debi still had her arm linked in his. 'I guess she figured if she caught my flu, she might even miss Halloween.'

At that, Debi bit her lip and lowered her eyes. For one frightening second, Daniel thought he'd somehow said something wrong, but then Debi lifted her pretty blue eyes up to him, giving a shy smile.

'Speaking of Halloween . . .'

Daniel held his breath. 'Yeah?'

'Well, let's just say I try not to let myself get carried away by the whole Halloween vibe,' Debi explained. 'I usually do something totally unrelated. Something completely candy-less and monster-free.'

Monster-free? That wouldn't include Daniel, then.

'Back in Franklin Grove, a few of my friends felt the same way, so we'd just skip the whole costume thing and head to a movie on October 31st.' She took a deep breath. 'I was wondering if you might like to join me this year?'

Daniel couldn't believe his wolf-ears. She was asking him to a movie? Now that *was* a real date!

He gave her a big smile. 'I would love to,' he said.

'Are you sure?' I know most people think it's one of the coolest nights of the year. I wouldn't want you to give up something you enjoy just to take me to the movies.'

Daniel gave his best 'casual' shrug, hoping he could convince her he wanted to go without letting on that he'd happily give up *breathing* if it meant he could take her to a movie.

'Well,' he began, 'I mean, there's nothing wrong with Halloween, but I've always felt the whole concept was kind of . . . um . . . *risky*.'

'Risky?'

'Sure. For example, say you're like out trick-or-treating and somebody gives you . . . uh, let's say an extra-chewy caramel chocolate bar, right? And say you decide to eat it right there on the spot and then, the next trick-or-treaters you run into are dressed in, like, the most terrifying costumes possible, like, say . . . mummified vampire zombie ghouls from Mars or something. And then you get all scared or whatever and you start screaming while you've got this big old glob of extra chewy caramel in your mouth. You could easily choke to death!'

'Wow,' said Debi, staring at him. 'I honestly never thought of that.'

Now she probably thinks I'm out of my mind!

'So, yeah,' he mumbled, dropping his eyes to his clashing shoes so she couldn't see his burning red cheeks. 'The point is, I'd be glad to hit up the movies.'

When he finally forced himself to look up at her again, he saw that her blue eyes were twinkling. 'Thanks, Daniel,' she said. 'I'm really looking forward to it.'

As they set off again through the crowds of people, Daniel was aware of a new swagger in his step. 'How about a bag of popcorn?' he offered. 'Or maybe a chocolate donut? You know, I could really go for a hot dog. And a couple of rare cheeseburgers would be good, too.'

Debi giggled. 'Sounds delicious.'

Beaming, Daniel led Debi in the direction of the food booths. Somewhere in the back of his brain, he had a feeling he was forgetting something really, really important – something about Halloween – but the thought didn't last long, because his brain was being overruled by his stomach.

'Cheeseburgers it is,' said Daniel. 'I'm starving.'

Suddenly, he had the appetite of a fully-fledged werewolf.

And the confidence of a boy on an actual, *real* date!

Chapter Three

Justin dropped into his chair at the kitchen table, pleased to see that Mom had set out an enormous Sunday breakfast before leaving to visit her sister. When he reached for the pitcher of orange juice, though, the movement sent a stab of pain into his left shoulder. Yesterday's hand-holding – with all the making sure he wasn't squeezing too tightly, dodging other fair-goers and occasionally saving Riley from major trip-and-falls – had resulted in *serious* arm cramps. Next time he'd have to remember to stretch out first.

At the moment, though, he had a much bigger

concern than the pain in his arm. Across the table, Daniel had his head in his hands and was groaning like a wounded animal. 'What's wrong?' asked Justin, piling his plate high with waffles. 'More girl trouble? Still not sure Debi likes you?'

Daniel took his hands away from his face. 'Debi asked me to go to the movies with her . . .'

'But that's great . . . isn't it?' Justin knew his twin could turn emo at the drop of a hat, but he always thought that when the girl you liked asked you out on a date, that was *good* news.

'. . . On Halloween.'

This was starting to make more sense.

Daniel winced. 'And I accidently said yes.'

'*What?!*' Justin nearly dropped his plate. 'But, Daniel, did you forget there's gonna be a *full moon* on Halloween night?'

Daniel helped himself to a slice of ham and some sausages. 'I seem to have this habit of getting a bit fuzz-brained whenever I'm with Debi. I . . . *forget* stuff, if you know what I mean.'

Justin knew *exactly* what he meant. He occasionally had that problem around Riley.

'Besides,' Daniel continued, '*you* try looking into a pair of big blue eyes like hers and saying no.' He shook his head hard. 'Impossible.'

'Yeah, I can see how it would be.' Justin grinned, thinking of Riley's dazzling brown eyes. He knew how helpless his brother must have felt. 'OK, so what are we gonna do about this?'

Daniel leaned back hard in his chair and dragged his hand down his face. 'That, brother, is a very good question. I barely slept worrying about it! Either I go with Debi to the movies and turn into a werewolf during the trailers, or I make some stupid excuse to back out, and blow my chances of ever getting her to be my girlfriend.' A tiny pup-like growl of frustration escaped his

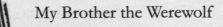

lips. 'Why does there have to be a full moon on Halloween? That's so lame!'

'Maybe the theatre will be so dark Debi won't even notice if you change,' Justin offered, although he really didn't think that was possible.

Judging by Daniel's expression, he didn't think so either. 'All I can do is hope for the best.'

'Hope for the best about what?' asked Dad, coming into the kitchen.

'Uh . . .' Daniel quickly stuffed two whole sausage links into his mouth and began to chew. 'Nuffin',' he muttered around the giant mouthful.

Dad frowned. 'Look, Daniel, just because you're a werewolf, it doesn't mean you can forget your table manners.'

Justin watched as Daniel gulped down the sausage guiltily. For a second he thought he might have to perform the Heimlich manoeuvre on his twin.

'Hey, Dad,' said Justin, pouring maple syrup on his fluffy Belgian waffle. 'I was wondering about Halloween. Is there any way that Daniel could just sort of, I dunno, *resist* turning? Can he fight it, and stay human if he wanted?' He noticed his twin give a hopeful glance. 'I mean, he's been getting really good at keeping it in check at school and stuff.'

'There's really no chance of that, I'm afraid,' said Dad, helping himself to a glass of juice. 'I'm proud of Daniel for being able to control his emotions so far. But a full moon – especially a full moon on Halloween – is another story entirely. Young werewolves have no chance of resisting its power. That takes years of practice.'

'That's what I was afraid of.' Daniel sighed.

'Besides, why would you *want* to resist?' asked Dad, sipping his juice. 'Halloween is a great night to be a werewolf! You can go out in public and everyone will think you're in costume. Once, your mom and I went to a Halloween masquerade ball and not only did we win the foxtrot contest, I also won best costume . . . and I wasn't even wearing one!' Dad laughed, grabbed a giant cheese Danish and left the room.

'So there's your answer,' said Justin. 'Just tell Debi you're wearing a werewolf costume to the movies.'

'Won't work,' said Daniel glumly. 'She already told me she doesn't really like the whole costume thing. She said she wanted a *monster-free* Halloween.'

'Oh.' Justin frowned. 'Well, that's a bummer.' Secretly, he thought the whole thing was kind of odd – what did Debi have against Halloween?

'I guess I'm just going to have to cancel on her.' Daniel sighed. Before Justin could say something comforting, the doorbell rang. Since Daniel was busy pouting over his strawberry waffle, Justin went to answer it.

He opened the door to find Kyle and the Beasts on his front porch, all of them grinning like they'd just made a spectacular play for a game-winning touchdown.

'A little early for trick-or-treating, isn't it, guys?' Justin joked nervously. He seriously hoped they weren't there to drag him off for an extra practice session – he wasn't sure his hand-holding muscles could take it.

'Just wanted to firm things up for Halloween, dude,' said Kyle. 'You'll be prowling with us that night.'

'I will?'

'Sure. It's a tradition.' Kyle reached out and landed a friendly punch on Justin's already aching shoulder. 'And it's mandatory. Coach Johnston considers it team bonding.'

'Team bonding with candy!' laughed Kyle's sidekick, Ed Yancey.

Justin thought back to the Halloween when a bunch of junior high boys in wolf 'costumes' had stopped him and Daniel in the street and demanded the boys pay the 'candy toll', before being allowed to continue on their way. He remembered they each sacrificed a peanut butter cup and a bubblegum lollipop before the boys had growled a bone-chilling 'thank you' and sent the twins on their way. Now it made sense: they must have been that year's batch of Pine Wood football Beasts, taking advantage of the holiday to let their inner wolves show.

'It's a blast,' Kyle assured Justin. 'We turn wolf, then go out on the town without having to worry about being seen by anybody. Total freedom, dude! It's gonna be awesome.' He narrowed his eyes and glared at Justin. 'We can just be *ourselves*.

I think *you'd* really dig that, wouldn't you, J-Man?'

Something about the way he said that made Justin cringe. Again, he had the feeling Kyle knew more than he was letting on.

'You in, dawg?' asked Chris Jordan, the tallest and burliest of the bunch.

'Of course he's in,' said Kyle slowly, not taking his eyes off Justin. 'He's one of us, isn't he?'

Justin gulped. 'You know it, dog – I mean, *dawg*!'

'Good,' said Chris. 'We'll head off at eight. Be ready to howl.'

Justin forced a big smile and accepted Ed's high-five. 'Wouldn't miss it! I mean, what's the use of having a secret identity if you can't use it, right?'

Of course the *real* secret was that Justin's identity actually belonged to his brother!

When the Beasts were gone, Justin closed the front door. He trudged back to the kitchen, where Daniel was clearing away the breakfast plates.

'So,' he began sheepishly, forcing a chuckle. 'About Halloween . . .'

'I heard everything,' said Daniel, pointing to his ears. 'Super-powerful wolf hearing, remember?'

'Right.' Justin flopped into a chair and sighed. 'Looks like we both accepted Halloween offers we shouldn't have, huh? I guess I'll just have to pretend I'm sick on Halloween night and tell the Beasts I can't make it.'

'*You* can't make it?' said Daniel, dropping a syrupy fork into the dishwasher. 'You mean, *I* can't make it. If they're expecting a fully furred-and-fanged out pack-mate for the evening *I* would have to be the one who was going.' He frowned. 'And then, you know, *not* go.'

''Splainy?' This was beginning to give Justin a headache.

'I can't go to the movies with Debi because I *will* turn, and you can't go prowling with the

Beasts because you *won't*. The only solution is that we both stay home.' Daniel knit his brows. 'Uh, I think.'

A wave of panic crashed in Justin's gut. 'Uhm . . . I kind of promised Riley I'd be a Creepy Caretaker, or a Scary Sitter, or . . . something.' He dragged his hands through his hair. 'If I'm out trick-or-treating with Riley and the Beasts see me in human form, I'm dead meat.'

Daniel crooked a grin at him. 'Well, at least we know they *like* dead meat.'

'Not funny, Bro.' Justin put his hands to his head like he had just missed the simplest of catches. 'They'll know I'm not a wolf.'

Daniel closed the dishwasher and sighed. 'Unless they see *me* out with Riley.'

'Huh?' Justin's head swam. 'I don't get it.'

'I barely get it myself,' said Daniel. 'But here's how I *think* it could work: I go out with the Beasts and pretend to be you. You go out with Riley and you also pretend to be you.'

'How do I "pretend" to be me?'

'Well, you won't actually be *pretending*, you'll just be pretending to *be* pretending if the Beasts see you. While I'm pretending to be you, you'll be pretending to be me pretending to be you. Got it?'

Justin shook his head. 'Not at all.'

'You go trick-or-treating with Riley as yourself. I go out with the Beasts, as you. If you happen to run into us, I'll just say that you're me – Daniel – pretending to be you – Justin – for Riley's sake.'

Justin closed his eyes and let the whole crazy plan sink into his brain. 'I think I'm having an identity crisis.'

'Tell me about it,' said Daniel.

'It's a good plan,' said Justin. 'Except for one thing. You still don't get to go out with Debi on Halloween night.'

'I know,' said Daniel glumly. 'And that stinks. But the only way we could have made *that* work is if we were triplets.'

Justin put a hand on Daniel's shoulder and gave it a grateful squeeze. 'Even if we were triplets, you'd still be the best brother in the world.'

The sounds of the cafeteria assaulted Daniel's wolf ears: spoons clattering, foil crinkling, and the curious whispers of the kids who were watching him with Debi, trying to determine if they were an official couple.

If you guys figure it out, he thought, *please let me know.*

From what he could hear (which was pretty much everything) the consensus was that they were almost on the verge of becoming a semi-official 'item'. Whatever *that* meant. He was so preoccupied with the whispers of the other kids, he was barely paying attention to what Debi was saying. He forced himself to tune in.

'. . . and then the cheer coach said to Mackenzie, "I'm sorry, Miss Barton, but I do not think that offering Look Like Your Favorite Cheerleader makeovers would be an appropriate fund-raiser for the squad."' Debi finished with a giggle and eye roll. 'Can you imagine it? Mackenzie Barton handing out pom-poms and making over every girl in Pine Wood until they were all exact clones of her?'

'Sounds like the plot of a horror movie,' Daniel observed. 'Attack of the Pom-Pom Posse.'

Debi laughed. 'That's one movie I'd never rent! You're so funny, Daniel.'

But even that compliment couldn't make Daniel feel less miserable. He simply had to break his date with Debi and there was no point in putting it off any longer. The stalling was making it all so much worse.

'Are you OK?' Debi asked, motioning to his untouched burger. 'You seem upset.'

Just say it. 'Well, see, the thing is, um, I'm not going to be able to go to the movies with you on Wednesday night.'

He braced himself for the reaction and looked at her.

Debi's eyes were filled with disappointment and it made something in his chest hurt. 'Why not?' she asked. 'Is something wrong? Are you sick?'

Yeah, sick of being a werewolf.

'No,' he said. 'I'm fine.' *If you can call being a fur-sprouting freak 'fine'.* 'I just have to do this . . . thing. It's kind of a family tradition. It means an awful lot to my dad. He's been doing it since he

73

was my age. So I really can't miss it.'

Well, at least everything he'd said was actually true. Vague and misleading, but he wasn't *lying* to her. He felt a little better. He might be a lousy 'almost semi-official-boyfriend' but at least he wasn't a liar.

'Oh.' Debi gave him a sad smile. 'Well, I totally understand. I mean, it's a family thing so of course you have to go.' Her eyes lit with an idea. 'Hey, maybe we can go to a later show, when you get back from wherever it is you're going.' She tilted her head. 'Where *are* you going, anyway?'

'Um . . .' Daniel felt his throat tightening. His ears began to itch and he had to concentrate extra hard to keep from wolfing out right there in the lunch room. Why had every location he had ever seen in an atlas fallen out of his head? 'Someplace.'

'*Someplace?*' she repeated, clearly hurt.

'Uh, yeah.' Daniel felt like the biggest creep in the world. 'But it's not that I *want* to do this stupid family thing. Honest. I'd much rather spend Halloween at the movies with you. Because, well, you know, because I *really* like . . .'

He was about to say he really liked *her* but stopped himself.

'. . . the movies,' he finished abruptly. 'I really like the movies.'

Ask her to go another time. Use that cheesy line about taking a rain check. Say something – anything – that will make her feel better.

But before he could say another word, a pair of pom-poms landed in the middle of the table. The pom-poms were followed by a lunch tray, which was followed by Mackenzie Barton.

'Hey hey!' she squealed in her uber-upbeat way. 'Don't you two look cozy!'

Debi looked away, and Daniel felt his heart crack.

'So Deb-a-licious, what are you doing for Halloween?' She blinked, tapping her chin. 'Wait. Did they have Halloween where you came from?'

'Mackenzie,' Daniel snapped, 'she's from a different state, not a different planet!'

'Oh, good!' Mackenzie clapped her hands. 'Then you know it's a total girl-bonding holiday. Cute costumes, lots of sparkly make-up, maybe a tiara. You could totally rock a tiara! *And* it's the one night of the year when girls can eat tons of chocolate candy and not have to worry about breaking out in spots because it's actually magical Halloween candy that doesn't give you zits.'

Where does she get her facts from? Daniel wondered.

'So?' Mackenzie prompted. 'Do you have plans?'

Debi looked at Daniel, held his eyes for one

second, then turned to smile at Mackenzie. 'Not any more.'

'Awesome! Then you can come. We're totally going to be the cutest trick-or-treaters ever and then we're going back to my house to have a little cheer party.'

'Thanks,' said Debi, standing up. 'I'm not really a fan of Halloween. But I guess I'll think about it.'

'What's to think about?' Mackenzie asked, truly shocked. 'I mentioned the tiaras, right?'

'I'll let you know,' said Debi, then her eyes landed on Daniel's again. 'Right now I have to go . . . *someplace.*' With that, she picked up her tray and left the table.

Daniel knew that remark was aimed directly at him. And it hit – right on target. *Ouch!* He watched her go, realising that now he was left eating lunch alone with Mackenzie Barton. Well, he supposed that was a suitable punishment – not only for ditching Debi, but for giving her such a lame excuse.

Mackenzie was shaking her head. 'I do not understand that girl.' She sighed, dipping her spoon into her fruit cup. 'I guess it's because she's a foreigner.'

'Mackenzie,' said Daniel through his teeth, 'people from Franklin Grove are *not* foreigners!'

'If you say so,' said Mackenzie. 'But what would *you* call a teenager who isn't totally excited to go out on Halloween?'

A werewolf, Daniel answered silently.

Chapter Four

'Yeehaw!'

It was Halloween night and the twins were standing in front of the bathroom mirror. Justin was already in costume, and he was wondering if he'd made a bad choice. 'Is a cowboy too dorky for a guy our age?' he asked, adjusting the ten-gallon hat on his head.

'Nah,' said Daniel. 'You look great.' He shot his brother a grin in the mirror. 'So when are you plannin' to mosey on over to Miss Riley's ranch? Gonna stop at the ol' saloon for a sarsaparilla first?'

Justin scowled as his brother cracked up at his own wit. At the moment, Daniel was mid-turn; he had a few scruffy patches of hair sprouting from his face and chest and his ears were only half-pointed, which made him look more like a scraggly mutt than an actual werewolf.

'Knock it off, Rover, or I'll drop you off at the dog pound on my way.'

Daniel stopped laughing abruptly and let out a wolfish whine that made Justin smile.

'Thanks again for doing this for me,' said Justin, his tone sincere. 'Wish I could have helped you out with Debi.'

Daniel shrugged as though it hardly mattered, but Justin knew he was upset because at the mention of Debi's name, his claws sprouted and his teeth grew into sharp fangs.

'When am I supposed to go meet up with the Beasts?' Daniel asked.

'They said they'd come and get you . . . er . . .
me . . . around eight o'clock.'

'So I'll just wait here alone,' muttered Daniel.
'And try not to eat all Mom's trick-or-treat candy.'

As Justin made his way down the stairs, he
knew he owed his brother big time.

He just had no idea how he could ever
repay him.

/// \\\ ///

On the front steps of the Carter's house, Justin
was about to ring the bell when he heard a loud
thud through the door. He peeked through the
window and saw Riley sprawled on the floor of
the front hall.

'You OK?' he called out.

'Fine,' she said, bouncing to her feet. 'Just
tripped over the hem of my costume.'

Two seconds later, the door opened and there was Riley, haloed in the glow of the porch light. Her hair was wrapped in a bright red silk scarf and she wore a white peasant blouse with puffy sleeves and ruffles around the neckline. Her skirt was also silk, long, flowing and splashed with every colour of the rainbow. Two huge hoop earrings hung from her ears and both her arms were adorned with a collection of jingly gold bracelets that went from her wrists to her elbows.

Justin blinked. She was a vision . . . of what, he wasn't totally sure.

'What are you?' he asked tentatively.

'I'm a gypsy fortune teller!' she announced, beaming.

'Aha!' he said. 'Where's your crystal ball?'

'Oh.' Riley shrugged. 'I had one, but I dropped it and it smashed.'

No surprise there. Justin didn't need a crystal

ball to predict his immediate future – he already knew he'd probably spend half the night catching Riley when she tripped over her skirt.

He also knew he was going to have the time of his life.

Suddenly, he was overwhelmed by an incredible idea.

It feels like the 'right time'!

He'd been thinking about kissing Riley for days now. They had mastered the hand-holding thing (more or less) and everyone in school knew they were a couple. Surely it was time that he kissed her?

It would be spontaneous and perfect. With the porch light glowing and the crisp autumn breeze ruffling the blonde strands that escaped from her headscarf, it was also going to be romantic. And he had less than five minutes before they were surrounded by their little chaperone-ees –

the opportunity would be lost.

So just lean in, and do it, Cowboy.

Girls on TV were always talking about how much they loved spontaneity and surprises. What could be more surprising than being kissed by a guy wearing a string tie and a ten-gallon hat?

Justin took a deep breath and moved towards her.

She moved towards him. *Good sign.*

He closed his eyes and . . .

'Ouch!'

Epic fail! Justin opened his eyes to see Riley rubbing her nose; the brim of his stupid hat had must have clonked her on it.

Stupid, stupid ten-gallon hat!

'I'm so sorry!' he blurted.

'It's OK,' said Riley, her bracelets jangling as she gently massaged the bridge of her nose. Unfortunately, the crisp autumn breeze picked *that* moment to turn into a full-on wind, blowing her long hair up into her face. 'Ouch,' she yelped again. Her hair was now tangled in her bracelets. This took several seconds of careful manoeuvring to put right, but eventually, she was able to free herself from her jewellery.

Justin felt like a big old western wash-out. He didn't remember any hat-meets-nose incidents in the movies.

As they walked away from Riley's house together, Justin tried to make himself feel better. *It could have gone worse,* he thought. *You could have tripped her with your lasso in the middle of a hug.*

'I thought you were supposed to be *spooky* chaperones,' said the little boy in the dinosaur costume. 'What's so spooky about a gypsy and a rodeo clown?'

Rodeo clown? Justin didn't like the sound of that at all!

They'd just arrived at the community centre where Riley was picking up the kids from the Reach Out programme – a charity that organised treats for kids who had a sick brother or sister. The minute Riley and Justin reached the reception, the four six-year-olds they were going to be chaperoning – two boys and two girls – had thundered out to greet them.

'He's not a rodeo clown,' said Riley sweetly, patting Patrick, the little dino, on his head. 'He's a cowboy!'

'Not just any cowboy,' said Justin, suddenly inspired. 'I'm the Sheriff in this here town. So y'all better behave yerselves.'

A little girl in a ballerina costume, Emily,

folded her arms across her chest. 'If you're the Sheriff, then why aren't you wearing a badge?'

'Well,' Justin bent down to Emily's height and replied in a stage whisper, 'because I'm undercover, little lady, that's why.'

Patrick the dinosaur and the two other children – Joel, who was dressed as a superhero, and a zombie girl called Tess – laughed.

Riley giggled, too, which made Justin extremely happy.

Mrs Donovan, the Reach Out coordinator, joined them on the porch. She was holding the hand of a one-year-old girl, and a little boy of about three clung to her leg.

'Hi, Riley!' Mrs Donovan said before turning to smile at Justin. 'I see you had the good sense to bring back-up. And handsome back-up at that.'

Riley blushed. 'This is my . . . um . . . this is Justin.'

87

Justin tipped his cowboy hat to Mrs Donovan and thickened his accent to say, 'Howdy, Ma'am. Sheriff Packer, law enforcement.'

Mrs Donovan laughed. 'It's so nice of you to volunteer to help us out on Halloween.'

'Our pleasure,' replied Riley.

'All part of the service,' said Justin, deciding to stay in character and tipping his hat. 'OK, li'l cowpokes: let's mosey on outta here!'

The kids cracked up and followed him down the steps.

Their first four stops went smoothly and Justin was beginning to enjoy his role as responsible chaperone. But when they got to the fifth house, things got a bit trickier. The superhero had a hissy fit and accused the ballerina and the zombie of getting extra candy. Soon all the children were arguing loudly amongst themselves and Riley was getting flustered. Thinking quickly, Justin saved the day by taking a fun-size candy bar out of his own treat bag and giving it to the superhero.

'Here ya go, little fella,' he said as he handed over the treat.

Riley beamed at him, which felt better than any sugar rush he would have got from any candy bar.

At their sixth stop, things really got crazy.

The house was decorated to look spooky and haunted. Emily the ballerina suggested they skip it, but the zombie wanted to get a closer look.

As they headed up the walkway, they could hear eerie-sounding laughter coming from inside the house. A giant plastic Frankenstein waved to them with one jerky mechanical arm and the entire front porch was enveloped in a hazy greenish fog.

'It's just a smoke machine,' Riley said soothingly, and Justin saw the dinosaur slip his hand in hers. 'And I'm sure that laughter is just a recording.'

'Don't be scared,' said Tess the zombie. 'We've got Sheriff Packer to protect us.'

At that, Riley gave Justin another broad smile.

Just as they reached the bottom porch step, there was a blood-curdling scream and a hooded figure dressed in black sprung out of the bushes wielding a bloody sickle. It was a Grim Reaper.

The little trick-or-treaters let out a collective shriek of pure terror.

'Ahhhhhh!'

'Help!'

Patrick the dinosaur was clinging to Riley for dear life, while the other three threw themselves at Justin, screaming and shivering.

The Grim Reaper – who was actually a seventh grader Justin recognised from school – was laughing his head off. 'What a bunch of cry-babies!' he scoffed.

'They're only six,' Riley scolded. 'That was *mean*!'

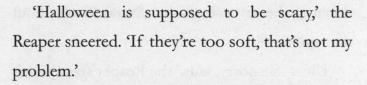

'Halloween is supposed to be scary,' the Reaper sneered. 'If they're too soft, that's not my problem.'

'Maybe it *is* your problem, pardner,' said Justin, deepening his voice and turning on the accent. He untangled himself from the trembling kids and took two long steps towards the prankster. 'Now, listen here. You done gone upset these little cowpokes. In fact, you plum scared 'em to death. I must insist that you apologise.'

The Grim Reaper, who was a good head shorter than Justin, looked up at him and gulped. 'You're one of the Beasts, aren't you?' he said, his bluster fading.

'I don't know what yer talkin' about, pardner. I'm just a humble lawman.'

'No, you're on the football team. You're Justin Packer.'

'That's *Sheriff* Packer to you, son.' Justin glared

down at the seventh grader. 'Now, how's about that apology?'

'Uh . . . s-s-sorry, kids,' the Reaper stammered. 'Didn't mean to scare you so bad. It was just a Halloween prank. You forgive me, don't you?'

'That depends,' Patrick piped up.

'On what?'

'On how much candy you give us!'

The Reaper immediately grabbed a huge bowl of candy from the porch and began dumping handfuls into all four bags.

'Good work, fella,' Justin drawled. 'Now, I reckon you won't be scarin' any more little cowboys and cowgirls tonight, will ya'?'

'N-n-no, sir,' said the Reaper. 'You reckon right.' Then he turned and bolted back into the house.

One crisis over, the kids skipped back towards the street, in time for Justin to have another moment of panic. The neighbourhood was crawling with ghosts, pirates, sports stars and storybook characters – which made it *truly* challenging to keep track of the kids. At one point, their dinosaur stopped to tie his shoelace and nearly got left behind. Then their little ballerina wandered off, but Riley managed to catch hold of her tutu just before she was accidentally swept away in a pint-sized pack of fairy princesses.

Once they had all four of their chaperonees back in line, Riley reached out and took Justin's hand. 'I meant to tell you, Sheriff Packer,' she said. 'You're a hero.'

'Well, thank you kindly, li'l lady. But I was just doin' ma job.'

'Look!' giggled the ballerina. 'Sheriff Packer and the gypsy lady are holding hands.'

'Ewww,' said the superhero. 'That's mushy.'

'I think it's nice,' replied the zombie.

'So do I,' Riley said.

Justin couldn't agree with her more. He was just about to tell her so when he heard some rowdy shouts coming from down the street.

'What now?' Riley asked. 'Who's making all that noise?'

When Justin saw who was causing the commotion, he grimaced. He was pretty sure his cowboy act wasn't going to work on *these* Halloween hooligans.

'My teammates,' he said grimly. 'The Beasts.'

They were close enough now that Justin and Riley could see their 'costumes'.

'Wow,' said Riley, a tremble of fear in her voice. 'They look really, really scary.'

They sure did! All of the Beasts had turned completely, which meant they were covered from head to toe in thick, shimmering fur. Their ears

were pointed and pricked up to hear every sound
for miles around. Their eyes were glowing slits
above their long, shaggy snouts and they all bared
their long blade-like teeth in the moonlight.

Even Justin shuddered a little. It was a freaky
thing to see.

But what was even scarier than those so-called
costumes was the thought of those wolf-boys
seeing Justin there with Riley. After all, he was
supposed to be pretending to be Daniel so that
Daniel could pretend to be him later on.

That could turn out to be a very awkward –
not to mention, confusing – conversation.

'Maybe you'd better take the little ones across
the street,' Justin suggested. 'I think after the
whole Grim Reaper incident, the last thing they
need is more scary costumes.'

'Good idea,' said Riley.

But when she let go of his hand to walk away,

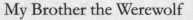

Justin felt a tug. *Uh-oh.* 'Wait,' he said. 'You can't go. I'm stuck on you.'

'That's so sweet. I'm kind of stuck on you, too.'

'No,' said Justin, pointing to his wrist. 'I mean I'm literally *stuck* on you. Your bracelet's caught on my sleeve.'

Sure enough, one of Riley's nine zillion bangles had snagged on the cuff button of Justin's plaid shirt. She gave it a little shake, but the bracelet held fast.

This isn't happening!

Justin glanced up from his button to see the wolves getting closer. His stomach clenched in a knot of pure dread. If Riley didn't get out of this fast, the Beasts would see them together and it would be harder to convince them that he was Daniel. After all, why would Daniel be out trick-or-treating with *Justin's* girlfriend?

'We've got to get unhooked,' he hissed, keeping his voice low because he knew the Beasts would be able to hear him soon, despite how far away they were. He shook his arm wildly in an attempt to free his button. All that succeeded in doing was making her bracelets jingle and jangle, which would surely catch the Beasts' attention. He abruptly stopped shaking his arm and froze in place.

'Are you ashamed to be seen with me or something?' Riley teased, taking advantage of Justin's stillness to try and work the bracelet free.

'Of course not. It's like I said – I don't want those guys to frighten the kids.'

He tried to disengage the bracelet by slowly lifting his arm over his head.

'Careful, I don't want to break it,' said Riley. She twisted her arm to the right. But still they remained linked together.

OK, I know I wanted to make a real connection with this girl, but this is ridiculous!

The Beasts were drawing nearer; Justin could hear their wolfish hoots and whistles.

'Hurry,' he said.

She stared at him, looking almost hurt. Immediately, Justin regretted snapping at her.

'I've almost got it,' she said. This time, when Riley twisted her arm to the left, the bracelet came away. And not a moment too soon.

'Go!' Justin said.

Riley looked confused. She frowned at Justin, then quickly herded their four children towards a well-lit house on the opposite side of the road. 'C'mon, kids. That's the McNeeleys' house. They give out king-sized candy bars!'

'Awesome!'

'Let's go.'

Riley and the kids had just stepped into the

shadows of the trees in the driveway when the Beasts reached Justin.

When Kyle spotted him standing in the middle of the road, he stopped in his tracks.

'Justin? Is that you?'

'Uh, yeah. I mean, *no*. I mean, well, sort of.'

'I think he's in a candy coma,' joked Chris. 'He can't even think straight.'

Justin had to admit that, up close, these guys were a pretty frightening crew. They could make anyone anxious with their sharp, gleaming teeth, their long claws, and their glowing wolf eyes. All of them were tall and muscular, and full of mischief.

And tonight was their night to prowl! They could howl at the moon and enjoy the rare feeling of the breeze in their fur without worrying that some human might become suspicious about their secret.

Halloween must be making everything worse, Justin realised.

Kyle was circling him now – like a real wolf, stalking prey. 'We were just on our way to your house to pick you up, dude.'

Justin forced a chuckle. 'Actually, you're on your way to pick up my *brother*. I'm Daniel.'

Kyle peered at him closely; Justin could almost feel the heat of his super wolf vision.

'You sure about that . . . Danny Boy?'

For one crazy second, Justin thought Kyle might actually ask him to prove he was Daniel, and how would he accomplish *that*? By bursting into song?

'Of course he's sure,' said Ed Yancey, smiling toothily. 'If he were Justin, he'd be –'

Chris cleared his throat loudly, cutting Ed off. 'He'd be dressed up in a wolf *costume*, just like us,' he finished, giving Ed a look.

'Oh, right,' said Ed. 'That's what I meant. Because, you know . . . that's the *rule*.'

Justin knew what he was referring to: older werewolves could hold back the transformation, but no werewolf their age could resist the power of the full moon – especially on Halloween.

'Still doesn't explain what Daniel's doing out with the J-Man's girlfriend,' said Kyle, narrowing his eyes.

So they saw me with Riley.

Justin's head started spinning as he thought of a good excuse. Hoping he sounded believable, he said, 'See, the real Justin's at our house, waiting for you guys. He didn't want his girlfriend to think he would break a date with her just to hang with his buddies. That's the great thing about being a twin – you can be in two places at once.' He eyed their fangs and smiled. 'Really cool costumes by the way,' he added, careful to keep a straight face. 'They look almost real.'

There, that ought to throw them off the scent.

'Dude, we're all about the authenticity,' said Caleb. 'And I'm glad your brother puts his teammates first. He's a true Beast.'

That's what you think, thought Justin. He was a becoming little unnerved by the way Kyle continued staring at him.

'So what's with the cowboy look, Daniel?' Ed asked. 'Couldn't you come up with anything scarier?'

The other Beasts laughed – except Kyle. The quarterback continued to look at 'Daniel' like he was a difficult question on a pop quiz.

'Uh, I'm not a cowboy,' Justin said, his brain suddenly clicking into gear. 'I'm a country–western singer!'

Caleb snorted. 'And that's supposed to be scary?'

'To a hardcore rocker like me it's about as scary as it gets!'

Thankfully, the Beasts laughed.

'Good one,' said Ed. 'I hate country music.'

.'I prefer heavy metal myself,' said Caleb.

'Country's almost as bad as techno-pop dance music,' Chris agreed.

But Kyle said nothing. He just continued to stare with his curious wolf eyes.

He knows, Justin thought, his stomach turning to knots. *I don't know how, but he knows I'm lying.*

'Anyway,' said Justin, 'you guys head on over to my house. I'm sure *Justin*'s got his costume on and is all ready to go out howling with you guys.'

'Howling.' Ed laughed. 'Yeah. That's what we do, all right.'

I'm an idiot! I'm not supposed to know they actually howl! 'I meant *prowling*.' He forced a chuckle. 'And by prowling, of course I mean you guys doing your jock thing . . . you know, having a blast and getting tons of candy. '

'Hey, that sounds like a good idea,' said Chris. 'My sugar levels are dropping. Let's go!'

With that, the werewolves headed off towards Justin's house, where Daniel, pretending to be Justin, would be waiting for them, fully wolfed-out.

With a huge sigh of relief, Justin crossed the street to meet up with Riley and the little ones.

'What was that all about?' Riley asked.

'Aw, they wanted me to hang out with them,' he said with a casual wave of his hand. '"Team bonding", you know? But I told them I had a way better offer.'

Riley smiled. 'They're nice guys, but sometimes their idea of fun is a little strange.'

Justin could only nod, thinking: *You have no idea.*

'Giddy-up, little pardners,' he said, slipping

back into his Sheriff persona for the kids. 'And thanks for being such good little deputies tonight.'

As they set off back towards the Community Centre, Riley laughed and reached for his hand. 'And thanks for being such a terrific boyfriend.'

Who needs candy when you've got the sweetest girlfriend in the world, thought Justin, not even caring that he was tangled in Riley's jewellery once again. *Yeehaw!*

Chapter Five

Daniel had to admit, there was an incredible sense of freedom in being able to wander the streets in all his Lupine splendour. Tonight, he didn't look any more peculiar than the goblins, mummies and rock stars parading through Pine Wood.

Of course, it didn't take long for him to become epically bored of hanging with the Beasts. There was only so much fun to have with a macho fest. All they seemed to want to do was punch and howl at each other – and they were *friends*. But for Justin's sake, Daniel went along with it, and punched and howled right back at the other wolves.

Kyle Hunter seemed to terrify any small pet they passed. Poor little cats and dogs would cower in fear when the quarterback strode past them, all except for a chubby, freckled cocker spaniel, which actually stood up and growled at him.

'Grr!' Kyle growled back, leaning down so he was nose to nose with the little dog. The quarterback was grinning, so Daniel knew he was just playing, but still – Kyle was letting a bit too much of his wolfishness show. *Maybe it's the Halloween effect*, Daniel wondered.

The spaniel gave a defiant yip, but eventually turned and scampered through the pet door, back into its house.

As the Beasts cracked up, Daniel resisted the urge to roll his eyes. *I'm glad Halloween only comes around once a year.* He made a mental note to stop by tomorrow with a nice meaty bone for the spaniel.

As the boys moved on, Kyle landed yet another jab on Daniel's shoulder. 'That dog looked almost as scared as your brother did when he saw us.'

Daniel gulped. 'You saw my brother?'

'Well,' said Kyle in a sly voice. 'It was either your brother or you. But how could it be you, right? I mean, you're a werewolf and he was dressed as a country-western singer. And he actually thought that was scary.'

Daniel shuddered. 'Well,' he said in a defensive tone, 'to a hardcore rocker, that's as scary as it gets!'

'Hmmm,' said Kyle, glaring at Daniel with his yellowish eyes. 'That's exactly what *your brother* said. Word for word, in fact. You scared of country singers, too, Packer?'

'Me? No way!' Daniel forced a laugh, but

something about the way Kyle was examining him made him think maybe the quarterback was beginning to suspect something. 'Hey,' he cried, changing the subject. 'Check out old Mr Hawthorne's house. No lights!'

He regretted it the minute he said it. Mr Hawthorne was a mean old guy and everyone knew it. If a kid ever hit a baseball or threw a Frisbee that landed in his yard, Mr Hawthorne would refuse to give it back. He was cranky all year round, but he was especially mean on October 31st. He did not like kids, and he did not like candy, and he *really* did not like kids knocking on his door and *asking* for candy!

For as far back as Daniel could remember, Mr Hawthorne had made this very clear to the neighbourhood trick-or-treaters by leaving his porch light off and his house dark on Halloween night.

Normal kids would just walk by and forget about it.

But Kyle and the Beasts were not normal kids.

'Let's leave it alone, guys,' Daniel said, trying to sound breezy. 'I hear the McNeeleys are giving out king-sized candy bars again this year.'

But the Beasts didn't hear him; they were too busy daring each other to ring Mr Hawthorne's bell.

Before Daniel knew what was happening, Kyle had bounded up Hawthorne's front steps and was ringing the doorbell – over and over again.

After a minute the door flew open. Even with his super wolf vision, Daniel could hardly make out the old man – he was bundled up in a dark, heavy bathrobe with a hood that hid his face. But even from the sidewalk Daniel could feel his annoyance. Daniel couldn't decide who was scarier – the werewolves or the grumpy old dude!

'Trick or treat!' cried Kyle in a phony, overly-cheerful voice.

Hawthorne didn't bat an eyelid at the sight of the wolf 'costume'. Instead, he let out a snort of disgust, then said in a deep voice, 'Get off my property.'

'No treats?' said Kyle in a pretend whine.

'No treats!' Hawthorne slammed the door so hard that Daniel jumped. He was pretty strong for an old guy.

'Mr Hawthorne needs to lighten up a bit,' said Kyle, his wolf teeth flashing in a wide grin. 'Who wants to see if we can make him laugh?'

Daniel felt a stab of panic. The Halloween effect had to be scrambling Kyle's sense of right and wrong. Curmudgeon or not, Mr Hawthorne had a right to refuse to take part in the holiday. And whatever Kyle was thinking, Daniel was pretty sure the old man wasn't going to find it amusing.

'What are you going to do?' Daniel asked, trying to sound casual, but he was already envisioning trees draped in toilet paper and a front door pelted with eggs.

'Don't sound so worried, Packer,' Kyle spat. 'Everyone likes pets, right?'

With that, Kyle lifted his head to the big white orb of the moon . . .

And he howled!

But this wasn't just any howl. This wasn't a friendly wolf-to-wolf greeting, or a howl of power and pride.

This was a summons.

The sound ripped through the night. All around them, Daniel could see trick-or-treaters stop in their tracks to see where the horrible noise was coming from. Older siblings and parents quickly guided the little ones away until only Daniel and the Beasts were left on the block.

But not for long.

Daniel's super wolf hearing picked up the sound of distant pounding, like a stampede. It was growing closer and closer.

The next thing Daniel knew, the entire street was filled with dogs of every shape, size and breed. Labradors and Retrievers, Shih Tzus and Chihuahuas, Dalmatians and German Shepherds. Even the brave Cocker Spaniel was part of the pack!

Daniel gaped as Poodles and Pomeranians, Collies and Cockapoos lined up on Mr Hawthorne's lawn, like cute little statues.

'That's what happens when you don't give treats.' Kyle laughed. 'You get great *tricks*!'

Daniel's head dropped as he sighed, wondering what the point of this was.

'C'mon,' said Caleb. 'Let's go to that house that gives out king-sized candy bars.'

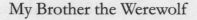

That was fine with Daniel. He wanted to get out of there and fast. But as he followed the Beasts down the block, he thought he sensed someone watching him.

He paused to glance over his shoulder back towards Hawthorne's house.

There, in the window, he could see Mr Hawthorne peeking out from behind the curtains. The hood of his robe had slipped back a bit and Daniel's heart thudded.

Were those fangs?

No. Of course not. It had to be just a trick of the moonlight, combined with Daniel's guilt over Kyle's rotten trick.

But had Mr Hawthorne's eyes always been so yellow?

In the next second, the curtain jerked closed and Daniel found himself running to catch up with the others.

Something told him he was in for a very long night.

Thankfully, the Beasts didn't pull any more 'great' tricks. They howled a lot, which seemed to unnerve the smaller children being led around by older brothers, sisters and parents; and whenever they found a bowl of candy left on a porch with a sign reading 'Please Take One', they helped themselves to at least five. Not exactly criminal behaviour, but still – Daniel wished they weren't being so obnoxious. Since he had discovered his wolf-gene, he had begun to resent a full moon. Tonight, he wished he could throw a giant blanket over it.

It was getting late, and the trick-or-treating traffic had thinned out considerably. Porch lights were being shut out, signalling the end of the candy provisions. They were only a few blocks from Daniel's neighbourhood, and they had the entire, dark street to themselves when Daniel's ears picked up a familiar voice, just coming around the corner.

Oh, no! Please let me be imagining things!

Not just any familiar voice, but one of his *favourite* voices.

Debi's voice!

What was she doing out on Halloween night? She'd told him she wasn't into it. But there she was, coming around the corner with the rest of her cheerleading squad, all of them wearing matching costumes – glitzy good witches in wispy white dresses with pastel sparkles and glittery wands.

And tiaras.

Daniel's heart flipped over in his chest. To

him, Debi looked more like an angel than a witch.

'Hey, look who's arrived,' said Caleb, training his wolf vision on the giggling gaggle of girls. 'Aren't some of those cheerleaders in your Homeroom class, Packer?'

'Uh . . . yeah.' Daniel swallowed hard. He was so thrown by seeing his crush that he spoke without thinking. 'Could you guys give me a little privacy for a minute? I need to talk to Debi.'

Ugh. Talk about putting his paw in it!

'Debi?' said Kyle, seeming suddenly alert. 'What do you want to talk to *her* for?'

Daniel was about to lie and say he had a homework question to ask her, but he realised that wouldn't require privacy.

'Isn't she the cheerleader your brother's been hanging out with?' Ed asked.

'Yes!' cried Daniel. 'Yes she is. Which is why I need to talk to her, in private. My brother –

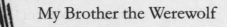

Daniel – is totally crushing on her and I need to tell her how he feels.'

'Daniel's crushing on Debi Morgan?' said Chris, in a tone of disbelief that made Daniel bristle.

'Yeah,' said Daniel. 'Why is that so hard to believe?'

Chris shrugged. 'I don't know.'

'What's that supposed to mean?' Daniel snapped. 'Daniel likes her, OK? A lot. He thinks about her all the time and they hang out and I'm pretty sure – uh – I mean, *he's* pretty sure she likes him, too. At least, I think he *thinks* she does.'

Chris held up his furry hands in surrender. 'Easy, dude. I was just surprised. Your bro seems kind of shy.'

Daniel felt his wolf anger rising. 'Well, what's wrong with that?'

'Nothin'.'

'I get it,' said Ed. 'Daniel really is shy, so Justin wants to put in a good word for his brother, right?'

Daniel nodded. 'Yep. That's what I want to do.' He peered around Chris and Caleb, seeing that the girls were getting closer. 'Would you guys mind putting a little distance between us? I mean, like, enough so that even your wolf hearing won't pick up what I'm saying?'

'Why?' asked Kyle, narrowing his eyes suspiciously.

'Um, well, because *Daniel* would be really embarrassed if you guys heard all the mushy stuff I'm going to tell Debi about him.'

'Yeah,' said Ed. 'Your brother does strike me as the kind of guy who likes to keep that stuff to himself.'

You have no idea.

Kyle stared at Daniel for a long moment, then

slapped his shoulder. 'I'm about ready to call it a night anyway,' he said.

Daniel smiled, relieved. 'Thanks, guys. I appreciate it.'

With that, the Beasts took off at a gallop. When they were out of sight – and sound – Daniel approached the group of girls.

'Debi?' he called tentatively.

They all turned, as perfectly coordinated on the sidewalk as they were on the sidelines. It occurred to Daniel that a pack of cheerleaders could be just as scary as a pack of wolves.

Maybe even scarier.

When they saw the terrifying wolf standing alone on the sidewalk, they all *shrieked*.

Do cheerleaders do everything in sync?

But Daniel noticed that of the twelve of them, Debi was the only one who didn't scream.

'Don't be scared,' he said, smiling and hoping

it didn't look too wolfish. 'It's me – Justin Packer.'

'Justin?' Mackenzie peered closely at him. 'Where in the world did you get that costume? It's . . . very convincing. And more than a little scary.'

'I, uh . . . made it myself,' said Daniel. *Not exactly a lie.*

'Well, what are you doing here?' Mackenzie demanded. 'You're supposed to be spooky chaperoning with Riley.' Her eyes lit up. 'Wait! What's the scoop? Did you two have a fight? Have you broken up?'

'No,' said Daniel. 'Nothing like that. The little kids had to get home early, so Riley went home and I met up with the guys from the team.'

'Oh.' Mackenzie seemed a little disappointed that there wasn't any 'scandal'.

'Listen, Debi, I was wondering if I could talk to you for a minute.'

Debi's eyes narrowed, looking curious. 'Sure,'

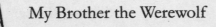

she said. 'I actually have to be getting home anyway. You can walk me.'

Debi said her goodbyes, and she and Daniel headed off in the direction of their street. Getting her alone to talk had seemed like a great idea five minutes ago, but now he was beginning to wonder if he *really* had the guts to go through with it. He'd hoped that impersonating Justin would give him the courage to ask Debi what her real feelings were, but now he realised that it was going to be a difficult conversation, no matter *who* she thought he was.

'That really is a realistic-looking mask,' she said, eyeing his furry face. 'Is it uncomfortable?'

In more ways than you know, Daniel thought. But he just grinned at her. 'I guess you could say it's grown on me,' he quipped. Daniel couldn't help a nervous laugh at his own joke. 'I thought you didn't like Halloween.' When she looked at him quizzically, he added, 'Daniel mentioned it.'

Debi shrugged. 'I really didn't want to come out, but Mackenzie can be very . . . insistent. Besides, since your brother bailed on me, I didn't have anything else to do.'

'I'm sorry about that,' said Daniel then quickly clarified, 'I mean, I'm sorry Daniel had to back out.'

'Well, it was really no big deal,' said Debi. 'Just two friends going to a silly movie.'

Daniel's mouth went dry. *Two 'friends'? 'Silly' movie?* So it wasn't a real date after all. 'Yeah,' he grumbled. 'That's what Daniel said.'

Suddenly, Debi frowned. 'Hold on – Daniel told me he couldn't go to the movies because he had a family obligation.'

'Right.'

'Well, last I checked, you two were in the same family. So why didn't *you* have to go to this mysterious family event?'

'Uh . . . you see . . .' Now he had *really* stuck his paw in it! Daniel wracked his brain to come up with a logical response. 'The event is this really big annual family dinner with all our aunts, uncles, cousins . . . basically everybody. Unfortunately somebody made a mistake and booked a very small restaurant for the party, so . . . uh . . . we had to go in shifts.'

'Shifts?' Debi echoed, her eyebrows knit in disbelief. 'For a family dinner?'

'Um, yeah. My dad and I took the early shift, and now Daniel and Mom are there.' He forced a laugh that almost came out as a howl. 'Me and Dad got to enjoy the appetisers, but Mom and Daniel get to have dessert.'

Debi looked away. She spoke under her breath, but Daniel's wolf ears picked up every word: 'So he *could* have spent some time with me earlier.'

The hurt in her voice made his stomach clench.

By now, they'd reached Debi's house. Daniel's wolf-ears picked up the sounds of Justin in his bedroom across the street, playing a video game. He hoped his twin had had a better time with Riley than Daniel was currently having with Debi.

'Thanks for walking me home, Justin,' said Debi sadly.

'Want me to tell Daniel you said hi?' Daniel asked hopefully. 'I mean, when he gets home from the late shift?'

Debi sighed. 'What would be the point?' Then she turned and walked into her house, leaving Daniel on the sidewalk feeling miserable and confused.

And *very* alone.

I must be cursed, he thought as he trudged across

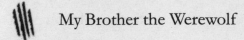

the street. *Or stupid. Maybe I'm both.*

How else could I manage to screw up my own love-life even when I'm disguised as someone else?

Chapter Six

Daniel stood in the cafeteria lunch line, feeling glum. His wolf stomach wasn't growling with hunger today. Even the special entrée – Extra Meaty Meatloaf with a side of barbeque spare ribs – didn't succeed in cheering him up. He was too bummed out to even think about food.

Two friends. Silly Movie.

No. Big. Deal.

Debi's words still haunted him. He'd tossed and turned in bed all night, replaying it over and over in his mind. He'd barely closed his eyes.

'Could you move it along?' A snippy voice from behind him brought Daniel out of his daze. He realised he'd been standing in front of the salad section of the line for what must have been a full minute, which was an eternity in lunch-line time. He turned to see Mackenzie Barton in the last stages of a long, exasperated huff.

'I've been sitting here watching my food wilt waiting for you to pick something,' she sneered, motioning towards the row of garden salads on the metal shelf.

'Oh, sorry.' Daniel reached for a plate of the day's meat-heavy special.

'Honestly,' sighed Mackenzie. 'Boys can be so clueless.'

She had a point. Daniel *was* clueless. And maybe, despite her ditziness, Mackenzie was just the person to clue him in. After all, she had spent the entire previous evening *with* Debi.

As he shuffled down the line to the dessert selections, he cleared his throat and aimed for a 'casual' tone. 'So, did you have a good Halloween?'

'Awesome,' said Mackenzie, dumping blue cheese dressing on her scraggly looking greens. 'I was a glam witch and I looked totally cute.'

'Did Debi have fun?' Daniel blurted.

'How did you know Debi was with me?'

'Um, well . . .' *Think, Daniel, think!* 'Justin mentioned that he ran into you guys . . . uh . . . you *girls*.'

Mackenzie shrugged, plucking a cup of butterscotch pudding from the shelf. 'I guess. Debi wasn't really into dressing up as a witch, though.'

'Really? But she looked great!' When he realised he'd almost blown his cover, he quickly added, 'I mean, you know, because she usually does, so I assume that she did last night.'

Mackenzie gave a smug sideways grin. 'Oh, you assume so, do you?,' she said in a teasing tone.

Daniel felt his face begin to burn. He grabbed a slice of apple pie and a carton of juice and wished he could just come out and admit that he did in fact really like Debi. *Yeah*, he thought, *and while I'm at it, maybe I'll just spill the beans about my werewolf alter ego, too.* Confessing to Mackenzie Barton was the equivalent of asking Principal Caine to reveal it over the loudspeaker during morning announcements.

But Mackenzie was right behind him. 'Look, Daniel, I might as well be straight with you. You don't have a chance with Debi Morgan.'

'What? Why?' Daniel stared at her. 'Did *Debi* say that?'

'She doesn't have to.' Mackenzie gave him a look that told him how utterly brainless she thought he was. 'Cheerleaders do *not* go for super-sensitive songwriters. They go for athletic boys. It's the whole point of *becoming* a cheerleader.' She rolled her eyes. 'Duh. It's practically a rule.'

Daniel frowned. 'Rules are made to be broken.'

Mackenzie gave an exaggerated sigh and began to walk away. 'So are hearts,' she called over her shoulder.

Daniel felt a surge of anger that had his teeth tingling. But under the anger was panic. Was Mackenzie right about this? His eyes scanned the cafeteria and found Debi, seated alone. Perfect. He'd sit down with her and make things right. Somehow.

But Mackenzie was already halfway to Debi's table. Daniel briefly considered turning on his wolf speed and bolting across the cafeteria, but that would only create more problems. Gritting his teeth (and willing them not to turn into fangs), he walked towards Debi's table, as calmly as he could.

Mackenzie had plopped herself down across from Debi, but Daniel noticed with some satisfaction that Debi didn't seem overly glad about her being there. This didn't stop Mackenzie from blathering on about what a great Halloween they'd had the second she'd taken her seat, though.

Daniel reached their table and for a moment, just stood there holding his tray. Neither girl seemed to notice he was there.

I can do this. I can sit down at a lunch table with the girl I like and have a conversation.

'Mind if I sit down?' he asked with a cheerful smile.

'Sure,' said Debi in a tone that was polite but cold.

Mackenzie was talking about how she'd

watched the Beasts wrestling in gym class that morning and how unbelievably hilarious Kyle Hunter was.

Rub it in, why don't you, Daniel thought, seething. He felt the itchy feeling of hair about to sprout on his arms and quickly unrolled his shirtsleeves to cover them up.

'He totally pinned Chris Jordan in every match. Kyle is the coolest. I mean, he is a jock, after all.'

So that's what cheerleaders want, is it? thought Daniel. *Competitive instincts? Macho coolness?* Weirdly, Daniel's recent transformation meant that he now *had* all of these things. All Daniel had to do was prove this to Debi.

But how?

Debi reached into her lunch bag and pulled out a bottle of strawberry-kiwi soda. Daniel watched as she struggled to unscrew the top.

'This doesn't seem to want to budge,' she

muttered, twisting the cap harder.

This was the perfect opportunity for Daniel to prove how strong he was.

'Here, let me,' he said, making an eager grab for the bottle. It flipped over twice before he got a firm hold.

'Wait!' said Debi, her eyes wide. 'Don't . . .'

Daniel gave the cap one good wolf-powered twist.

Spppppzzzzzzztttttttttzzzzzz!

The fizzed-up soda came spewing out of the bottle like a strawberry-kiwi geyser. The girls shrieked as a gush of pink liquid filled the air then rained down, splattering the table and the floor, soaking Debi, Mackenzie and their lunches. Mackenzie was flailing and wailing as though she'd been showered with scalding water rather than a fizzy drink.

Debi just sat there, stunned. Then, taking

what felt like the rest of the week, she slowly lifted her hands to her face and began wiping the soda from her eyes.

No one said a word.

Then Mackenzie began screaming at the top of her lungs. 'Daniel Packer, are you out of your mind? Who shakes up a bottle of soda before they open it?'

He wanted to say he hadn't really shaken it, not on *purpose* anyway. His wolf-strength had come on too strong and, unfortunately, it was the soda that paid the price.

'This sweater is genuine faux-cashmere,' Mackenzie roared. 'Not to mention a *high quality* designer replica! And now it's soaked.'

Daniel had never felt like such a loser in his whole entire life. He opened his mouth to apologise but the only sound that came out was a wolfish whimper.

135

'It's *ruined*, Daniel,' Mackenzie cried, loud enough for everyone in the cafeteria to hear her. 'Do the words "dry clean only" mean *anything* to you?'

They didn't, actually. Still, Daniel figured he should probably at least try to help clean up the mess he'd made. His eyes searched the table for a napkin, but before he could locate one his wolf hearing picked up another sound breaking through the ear-splitting noise of Mackenzie's shrill ranting.

'Justin was *where* on Halloween night?'

It was Riley's voice, shooting into his ear from the other side of the cafeteria. Daniel whipped his head around and saw her; she was talking to Caleb and Ed at the jock table. And she looked very, very confused.

'I just told you,' Ed was saying. 'He was out with us. And we had a total blast. Justin's pretty cool.'

136

Suddenly, Caleb gave Ed a sharp elbow to the ribs. 'Shhh,' he whispered, so Riley couldn't hear, but Daniel heard him as clearly as if he were standing right next to him. 'Justin had his brother fill in for him with Riley, remember? She was with *Daniel* all night. She didn't know Justin was out with us.'

Ed looked instantly guilty. 'Wait, did I say Justin was with *us*? What I meant to say was . . . uh . . . Justin was with you. And he told us you two had a blast. Together. On Halloween.'

Nice try, Ed.

Riley was frowning slightly, and Daniel couldn't tell whether she was confused, hurt or just plain angry. In any case, she just turned away from the Beasts and hurried out of the cafeteria. Daniel immediately went after her.

He took two tentative steps towards the door before he remembered he'd been trying to work things out with Debi. Feeling torn, he turned back to the table to see that she was attempting to pick up her soda-saturated sandwich; it was so wet that it simply fell apart in her hands and landed in a mushy lump in her lap.

'Don't even *think* about leaving, Daniel Packer!' Mackenzie commanded. 'You made this mess, the least you can do is stick around to help clean it up.'

Daniel froze. *What do I do?!*

If he went after Riley he'd at least have a shot at fixing his brother's relationship. But leaving Debi now, with a lap full of soggy sandwich, would probably ruin any chance he ever had of working things out with her.

Not that he *had* a chance, according to Mackenzie's Cheerleaders-Love-Jocks theory.

Justin's relationship was worth saving, Daniel's was non-existent. His choice was depressingly easy.

'Sorry,' he said, letting his eyes meet Debi's for the scantest of seconds. 'I've got to go.'

Mackenzie let out an appalled gasp as Daniel took off at a run. He could still hear her insulting him even after he was out the lunch room and into the hallway:

'I can't believe Daniel Packer! He's being a real creep. Do you think he sprayed us with that soda on purpose?'

Of course I didn't. Debi has to know that.

But to his misery, Debi's reply was, 'I really don't know. Maybe.'

Daniel's heart sank. So Debi actually thought he could be *that* much of a jerk. Well, why wouldn't she? He'd totally ditched her on Halloween, for no good reason – at least, no good reason that he could *tell* her. For all she knew, Daniel was a thoughtless idiot who thought it was fun to randomly spray girls with soda.

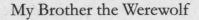

Focus, Daniel! Focus on Riley.

But Riley was nowhere to be seen. She'd disappeared and Daniel couldn't guess whether she'd taken the east corridor towards the gym, or the west, towards the science labs. Or maybe she'd just ducked into the nearest bathroom to sulk.

All things considered, that didn't seem like such a bad idea to Daniel.

Justin felt a hand clamp around his wrist. He looked up from his locker to see Riley glaring at him.

So is this some new style of hand-holding or am I in trouble?

The next thing Justin knew he was being dragged away from his locker and into an empty classroom.

OK. It's beginning to feel like trouble!

As Riley pulled him to the far corner of the room, she bumped into a desk, tripped over a book and nearly crashed into the wastebasket.

'Riley, what's wrong?'

'OK, Packer, let's hear it!'

'Hear *what*?' Justin was surprised to see his girlfriend so agitated. More to the point, he had no idea why she would be this upset with him.

'The truth, that's what!' Riley folded her arms across her chest. 'Ed said you were out with the football players last night. But I know for a fact that you were with me.'

Justin opened his mouth to answer, but she cut him off.

'And don't go trying to tell me that you and Daniel switched places, because I know you twins better than just about anyone. I mean, c'mon, how could I not recognise my own boyfriend!?'

Justin couldn't help grinning at that – but he did his best to hide it.

'Obviously,' Riley continued, 'Daniel was the one who dressed up in a wolf costume and went out with the Beasts. Right?'

'Yeah.' Justin sighed. 'But don't be mad. I wanted to spend Halloween with you, and that was the only way. The Beasts said prowling together was a mandatory "team-bonding" thing, so I couldn't just not show up.' He gave her a wary smile. 'Lucky for me I have an identical twin who could show up *for* me.'

'Did you force Daniel to do it?' Riley demanded. 'Did you make him break his date with Debi, just so you could keep yours with me?'

Justin wished he could tell Riley the truth. It broke him in two that he had to lie to her, but what would he have said? *Daniel couldn't*

142

*have kept his date with Debi because he was guaranteed
to turn wolf that night.*

No. Way.

So he just said, 'It's way more complicated
than that. But you've gotta believe me, Riley – I
didn't force him. He volunteered. Kind of.'

'"*Kind of* "?' Riley shook her head sadly. 'Was it
really so important to you to keep up appearances
with those obnoxious jocks that you'd let your
brother sacrifice his own Halloween plans? Not
to mention hurting the girl he really likes!'

Since when does a guy get in this much trouble for
keeping *a date with his girlfriend?* 'Daniel wanted to
do me the favour.'

'Well, you shouldn't have let him! You could
have explained to me that this silly outing with
the Beasts was a team requirement – I would
have understood.'

'I'm sorry,' Justin mumbled, dropping his eyes

to the floor. He was sorry for lying to her, but also feeling a little hard done by – it wasn't like he really had a choice. Justin sighed. Having a werewolf for a brother wasn't all it was cracked up to be.

'Debi's the one you should be apologising to. She was crushed when she found out that Daniel lied to her.'

Justin smiled in spite of himself. *Crushed?* 'So she must really like him then.'

'Are you blind? Of *course* she likes him!' Riley was almost shouting now. 'Or, at least, she *did* like him. She might feel differently now. And it's all your fault for being selfish. Why would you do that to Debi and Daniel?'

The look of disappointment in Riley's eyes nearly floored Justin as powerfully as a fierce tackle on the football field. He didn't want her to think he was selfish, or cruel. But he couldn't tell her the truth.

So all he could do was shrug. 'I dunno.'

'That's it?' gasped Riley. 'That's all you have to say? You're not even going to try to explain yourself?'

I wish I could.

After a long, uncomfortable silence Riley shook her head. Without a word, she turned and stormed out of the room, leaving Justin alone.

Miserable, confused, and alone.

Chapter Seven

The last thing Justin wanted to do was go to football practice. But rules were rules.

So he suited up in the locker room and trudged out to the field with the rest of the team. As they pounded through their warm-up he was barely aware of what he was doing. His mind was still filled with Riley's disappointed words. He could practically feel her accusing eyes on him, even as he counted out his jumping-jacks.

As always, the track around the football field was dotted with random spectators – a few teachers, some parents, a couple of scout-coaches from other schools, and a whole bunch of giggling girls.

Justin did a quick scan of the track, looking for Riley, just in case she'd decided to come watch him practise. But she was nowhere to be seen.

He finished the warm-up with a knot in his stomach.

And things got even worse when he went out to run through a passing drill.

Kyle threw a long, sizzling spiral that split the air like a rocket. Justin ran hard and fast, arms pumping and feet thundering across the field. By some miracle, he caught the ball; by pure instinct, he started running.

And running . . .

It's all your fault for being selfish.

And running . . .

Why would you do that to Debi and Daniel?

And *running* . . .

And *WHAM!*

Justin opened his eyes to see a hazy version of Kyle Hunter hovering over him.

'Dude! You still breathing?'

'Huh?' Justin blinked, trying to focus. His head throbbed. His back hurt. And the whole world seemed to be going in circles. 'What happened?'

'You made it to the end zone,' Caleb explained, laughing. 'And then you tried to find a place *beyond* the end zone.'

'Yeah,' said Ed. 'Good thing that brick wall was there or you'd probably still be running.'

So I slammed head first into a brick wall?

That still didn't feel as bad as hurting Riley felt.

Kyle's voice broke through Justin's foggy thoughts. 'How many fingers am I holding up?'

'Uh . . . eleven?'

Billy Tate, the first string defensive back, laughed and offered Justin a hand up. 'The

148

answer is "no fingers". That's Kyle's favourite joke. He did it to me once when I came to after crashing into the goal post. He scared the life out of me. I thought I'd gone blind.'

As they made their way back to the bench, Kyle dropped a muscular arm around Justin's shoulders. 'Way to go, faking an injury for the spectators,' he said, impressed. 'Keeps people from guessing our *secret*.' He chuckled. 'Next time, though, hold back a little. You don't have to actually pretend to be unconscious.'

'Good to know. Thanks,' Justin mumbled. His head was pounding and he felt a little queasy. The November sky was already getting dark and a plump golden moon was teasing them from behind the treetops.

'Let's call it a day, guys,' said Kyle. He motioned to the moon and lowered his voice. 'It's still close enough to being full that a few of us might turn.

Don't want the spectators spectating *that!*'

Justin couldn't have been more relieved. He changed out of his uniform in record time and headed home.

When he arrived, he immediately called out for Daniel. 'Yo, Bro. You home?'

'Daniel's not here,' said Mom, appearing in the hallway and wiping her hands on her apron. 'Don't you remember? It's Thursday. His band is rehearsing at school.'

Justin felt an explosion of panic. He hadn't had a chance to tell Daniel about his confrontation with Riley, so Daniel was unaware that his lead singer knew all about the Halloween switch. If Riley approached Daniel about it, who knew what he'd do? He was so upset about Debi he just might crack and confess *everything*.

OK, so it was Daniel's secret to tell, but even a non-wolf like Justin knew the rules. Telling humans about the werewolf world was, if not strictly forbidden, then strongly frowned upon.

Justin was just going to have to get to Daniel before Riley had a chance to 'Rile' him up.

'I have to go, Mom,' Justin said, picking up the jacket he'd just dropped on the floor.

'But you just got home.'

'I know, but, uh . . . I forgot my history text-book. And you know what they say – those who forget their history books are doomed to repeat the class.' He gave his mother a wave as he bolted out the door.

But Justin had much more important things to worry about than his history grade.

His twin brother might be on the verge of spilling a very big secret. A secret that might freak out Riley, and put an end to her wanting to have anything to do with either Packer twin.

If Daniel decided to tell Riley about their

werewolf heritage, it just might be Justin's relationship that turned out to be history!

The guitar solo had just reached its seventh minute – and the extended instrumental finish still had six and a half minutes to go.

In Sheep's Clothing were rocking the empty school auditorium with the 'outro' to a song Daniel and Nathan, the bass player, had written, called 'Souled Out'. The wiry growl of Daniel's guitar echoed through the vast room. Riley, their lead singer, sat on an amp, with *nothing* to do during the long riff. Nothing to do, except stare right at Daniel.

And it was beginning to freak him out.

Why did she look so angry? Had she heard he'd cancelled his and Debi's Halloween date?

Was this some kind of 'girl-power' united front?

Daniel felt the will to play drain out of him, like a plug had been pulled. He dragged his finger across the strings to send one last screech ricocheting through the room. Then, silence.

'What are you doing?' Nathan demanded. 'You've got, like, at least five more minutes of noodling still to go.'

'Yeah,' said Otto. 'You've still got oodles of noodles . . . dude-les.' Then he hit his drums to mark his 'joke' –

Buh-dum-bum, tsh!

'Not in the mood to noodle,' Daniel muttered. 'I've reached my noodle limit.'

'C'mon man!' barked Nathan. 'This whole rehearsal's been a waste of time.' He pointed his plectrum at Riley. 'Your vocals were all over the place. You forgot the lyrics to three of the songs and you kept changing keys.'

'I guess I just have other things to think about.' Riley huffed.

'What else is there to think about?' Nathan demanded, shaking his head so that the dyed stripe in the middle of his hair waved like a purple flag. 'What's more important than rock 'n' roll?'

'Lots of things,' said Riley, levelling a look at Daniel. 'Like honesty. And loyalty.'

'Daniel, we have to talk.'

Daniel's head snapped up at the sound of Justin's voice in his ear. But when he looked around the auditorium, his twin was nowhere in sight.

Wolf hearing. OK, so where was Justin? Outside the auditorium? At home in bed? On the moon, maybe? It was hard to judge.

'I agree with Nathan,' said Otto, twirling a drumstick between his fingers. 'We sucked today. Big time. We've only had one gig and that was

154

Homecoming. I seriously hope we didn't peak already.'

'That would make us one-gig wonders,' Nathan fumed. 'Nobody aspires to be a one-gig wonder!'

Glad to have an excuse to call it a day, Daniel said, 'Let's pick this up again tomorrow.' He removed his guitar strap from his shoulder.

Muttering under their breath about 'creative differences', Otto and Nathan collected their things and stomped away, leaving Riley and Daniel alone in the auditorium.

She sprang off the amp and began packing up her book bag.

'Look,' said Daniel, 'I'm not sure why you're so upset, but if it's because rehearsal didn't go well, don't worry – every band has off days.'

'This has absolutely nothing to do with rehearsal,' said Riley. 'This is about what you and Justin did to Debi.'

Daniel felt the backs of his hands begin to itch; he quickly jammed them into the pockets of his jeans. 'Oh.'

'Debi was *so* upset,' Riley informed him, swinging her backpack on to her shoulder with a little too much gusto; the motion sent her spinning around. Luckily, she managed to catch herself before crashing into the drum kit.

'Was she?' Daniel asked, frowning. 'Because her exact words were, "No big deal".' That annoying little phrase had been burrowing through his brain like an earworm since the minute Debi had said it.

Riley rolled her eyes. 'What was she supposed to say? That she was really hurt that you broke your date?'

So it *was* a date? Daniel felt a wave of sheer joy, despite the fact that Riley was telling him off.

'Quit smiling, Daniel!' Riley scolded. 'You

did a really crummy thing.'

'I know, it was terrible,' Daniel agreed, still smiling.

'You played with her feelings!'

'But I didn't mean to. It just . . . really couldn't be helped.'

Riley planted her hands on her hips. 'What does that mean?'

Daniel's smile faded into the silence, and Riley let out a snort of exasperation. 'Your brother couldn't seem to explain it either,' she said. 'Which is why I'm not overly thrilled with either Packer twin right now! In fact, I'm getting a little fed up with you two and your "big secrets".'

Daniel was such a jumble of feelings right now. He was happy that Debi had considered their movie plans to be a real date, but he was furious with himself for breaking them. He was torn between just blurting everything out to Riley – she was one of his oldest friends, after all – and just letting her believe he was a jerk who messed girls around. He was *so* torn, his teeth began to tingle.

He glanced up towards the high windows along the auditorium ceiling and saw the big, round one-day-past-full moon shining in the twilight sky.

Uh-oh.

'Listen, Riley, maybe we should continue this conversation some other time.'

'No, Daniel Packer. You need to explain yourself!'

'Daniel, where are you? Otto and Nathan came out of the auditorium five minutes ago!'

Daniel nearly jumped out of his skin when he heard Justin's voice again. He'd totally forgotten his brother was somewhere nearby, trying to talk to him.

'Riley didn't come out either,' Justin was saying,

'*so I assume you guys are having a talk. Well, let me clue you in . . . she already knows you covered for me with the Beasts last night!*'

'Sorry, what?' Daniel said back. If Riley knew, then –

'I *said*,' repeated Riley, fuming so much she looked like a blonde-haired kettle, 'you need to explain yourself!'

'*And I'm pretty sure now she's going to want to know why!*' Justin continued.

'Duh, I'm not stupid, Bro,' Daniel muttered under his breath.

'I think you *might* be stupid,' said Riley. 'And I'm *not* your "Bro".'

Daniel gave her a wobbly smile. 'Uh . . . yes . . . I know . . . I mean –'

'Or perhaps you would like to tell me what you were thinking?' said Riley, who was tapping her foot now.

'*Tell her you really like Debi,*' Justin suggested from wherever he was. '*Tell her you really wanted to go out with her but you couldn't because you suddenly broke out with a case of twenty-four-hour acne!*'

'Are you *crazy*?' Daniel blurted loudly. 'I'm not going to tell her *that*!' He immediately winced. To Riley, it must have looked like he was hearing voices in his head.

Which, Daniel supposed, technically, he was.

In a heartbeat, Riley went from looking angry to looking concerned. She was staring at him with wide eyes. 'Daniel, you're starting to scare me. Are you OK?'

'*Dude, don't blow it,*' came Justin's voice in his ear.

'Shut up!'

'I'm sorry, I didn't mean –' Riley started to back away from him, raising her hands as if asking him to calm down.

'No, no, no,' said Daniel quickly. 'I wasn't speaking to you.'

'Oh.' Riley blinked nervously. 'Then who *were* you speaking to?'

'Um . . .' Daniel looked around desperately for inspiration. Suddenly, it came to him. He did care about honesty and loyalty, just like Riley said. *The truth will set you free* . . . Who said that? Elvis?

Daniel sighed. He knew what he had to do. 'Justin, get in here,' he said in a normal voice.

Riley whipped her head around, scanning the auditorium. 'Daniel, Justin's not *here*.'

'Oh, right!' Daniel's brain was so muddled and confused he'd actually forgotten that the super-hearing deal wasn't a two-way street.

'Maybe we should call your mom,' Riley suggested, her eyes filled with worry. 'Do you want to lie down or something?'

'I'm fine,' Daniel assured her. Then he stuck two fingers in his mouth and let out a loud whistle, which he followed with a shout, 'Justin!' The name echoed in the empty performance hall. But then the door at the back of the auditorium opened and Justin stepped inside.

Riley's eyes flew open. 'How did you know Justin was waiting out there?'

'I heard him talking,' Daniel answered truthfully.

'From out in the hallway?'

Daniel nodded.

'Oh. So now you're not just keeping secrets, you're lying to my face, too?' She planted her hands on her hips. 'And a ridiculous lie, as well! What next? You're really a superhero?'

Daniel couldn't blame her for being upset. 'Listen, Riley . . .' he began.

But before he could explain, she turned away

from Daniel to face Justin. 'There's something very weird going on here,' she said.

'You've got that right,' sighed Justin. He glanced beyond Riley to meet his brother's eyes.

This time, Justin didn't have to speak to make his thoughts clear, because Daniel knew they were thinking the same exact thing. The twins shared a quick nod. Riley kept her back to Daniel as she folded her arms.

She did not see Daniel's hair and nails grow. She did not see the transformation.

'I want to know what you two are up to,' she said.

'Riley . . .' said Justin.

'I refuse to let you two keep hiding things from me. After all —'

'Riley,' said Daniel. 'Riley, turn around.'

Riley turned slowly back to face Daniel.

Then her hand flew to her mouth to stifle the

scream that sprang from her throat. Her eyes went completely wide as she stared at him, her face turning a ghostly shade of pale.

'You're a . . .

'But no . . .

'That's impossible . . .

'You can't be . . .'

'Riley,' said Justin. 'I'd like you to meet my brother . . . the werewolf.'

Chapter Eight

The moon cast a pale light on the front of Riley's house where she and Justin sat quietly, side by side in the porch swing.

They'd been sitting there for what seemed like forever, and still Riley hadn't said a word. A few times she'd opened her mouth as though she might make a comment or ask a question. But each time she'd just shaken her head and closed her mouth again.

Justin understood completely that she would need some time to process what she had seen.

It was a *lot* to take in.

Besides, it was nice sitting this close to her in the moonlight.

Somewhere in the distance, something howled. Riley jumped and clutched at Justin's arm.

'Was that . . .?'

Justin shrugged. 'Probably,' he said. There was no reason to lie to her any more, and he kind of liked it.

'It's so . . . *fantastic*,' Riley said. 'Not as in "cool", or "awesome", but as in . . . unbelievable.'

Justin agreed, glad she was still holding his arm. 'But true.'

'I guess I've always known there was something weird about Pine Wood, but I never would have guessed *this*.' A little shiver passed through her and she turned her brown eyes to Justin. 'Are they dangerous?' she whispered. 'The wolves, I mean.'

'Nah,' Justin assured her. 'I mean, they look

scary, but they're pretty domesticated.' He chuckled. 'They're just like humans – most are nice, and some aren't so nice.'

'Why aren't *you* a werewolf?' Suddenly, her eyes widened and she gasped. 'Wait. You're *not*, are you?'

'No, I'm not. It's kind of a long story.'

Riley's hand moved down Justin's arm to take his. 'I've got time,' she said.

So Justin told her everything.

He told her about the day his father had sat him down in the study for a '*serious talk*'.

'I thought maybe we were moving to Antarctica or something crazy like that. But it turned out the talk was about wolves.'

Riley considered this for a moment. 'Why did your father assume it would be you and not Daniel?'

'Because one of the signs of a werewolf is

exceptional athletic ability when in human form.' He realised how that sounded, and felt a blush creeping into his cheeks. 'Sorry, that sounded really arrogant, didn't it?'

'You're just telling the truth,' Riley replied.

He went on to tell her how disappointed he'd been when he realised that, despite his sports talents, he wasn't going to be a werewolf after all. And how freaked out Daniel had been the night of their thirteenth birthday, when he'd suddenly grown fur and sprouted claws.

Riley gave the swing a little rock and sighed. 'It must have been horrible for Daniel, turning into a wolf without having had any warning.'

She interlocked her fingers perfectly with Justin's, giving his hand a squeeze. He thought back to the Fall Fair, when he'd been so nervous about holding her hand. Now, it felt completely normal.

He was glad that at least *one* thing in his life felt that way.

'Sometimes you wish it had been you, don't you?' she asked softly.

Justin nodded, amazed. She *really* knew him! 'Sometimes I think it would have been cool,' he said. 'It would have made me a football star anyway.'

'You *are* a football star. You're *my* football star.'

That's pretty much the best thing anyone has ever said to me in my whole life.

Now Riley was looking up at him and her eyes were shining in the moonlight. She smelled terrific, like some kind of flowery shampoo and perfume that had a soft vanilla scent. The swing rocked gently beneath them and there was no one for miles around.

It was such a perfect moment that Justin couldn't have stopped himself even if he wanted

169

to . . . And he definitely didn't want to.

He closed his eyes . . .

Leaned in . . .

And kissed her!

'That's for being the best girlfriend ever,' he whispered, then placed another quick little kiss on the tip of Riley's nose.

She giggled. 'And what was that one for?'

'For not thinking I'm some kind of freak for being part of a werewolf family.'

'We're all kind of weird, aren't we?' she whispered.

They sat quietly for another moment, but it was getting late for a school night and they both knew it. Reluctantly, they said goodnight.

When Riley went inside, Justin waited until the front door closed behind her before heading down the porch steps. He'd never felt so content in his life.

He was just thinking about breaking into a crazy little happy dance when he spotted two figures lurking across the street.

Kyle Hunter and Caleb Devlin.

And from the looks on their faces it was pretty clear that they'd heard everything. Well, of course they heard everything – they were werewolves!

Justin took a deep breath and crossed the street to join them.

'Guess you guys want an explanation, huh?'

Kyle shook his head. '"Terrified of country-western music",' he muttered. 'I had a feeling that something was off that night. You and your brother have been trading places all along, making us look like fools . . .'

'So what are you going to do?' Justin asked, willing the fear out of his voice.

'I'm gonna have to think about it,' said Kyle.

171

'As Captain, I have to think about how this affects the team.'

'Meet us after practice tomorrow,' Caleb said, looking serious.

With that, the two Beasts turned and marched off into the darkness. Justin watched them for a minute, then he turned and headed home wondering how, in just a few minutes, his night had gone from awesome to . . . whatever the extreme opposite of awesome was.

'It's the right thing to do.'

Daniel stood at the end of the walkway, shovel in one hand, hedge trimmers in the other. He knew he was taking a chance, but this was something he had to do.

Thanks to Kyle's silly Halloween prank, old

Mr Hawthorne's yard was a bit of a disaster area. The shrubs and plants had been damaged by the dogs Kyle had summoned – they had clearly got bored of playing 'statues' some time after the Beasts had left and decided that digging stuff up was more fun. So Daniel had disguised his wolf self with a bulky hood and a pair of gardening gloves, and walked the three blocks back to Mr Hawthorne's house.

He set to work. Above him, the moon shone its pale light while he clipped and trimmed, cleared and re-planted.

'I had a feeling I'd be seeing you again,' came a voice from the porch.

Daniel looked up to see Mr Hawthorne on the top step. The old man was again bundled into his bathrobe, and looking at Daniel with a stern expression. 'You're right,' he said, eyes gleaming strangely yellow in the dark. 'It *is* the right thing to do.'

'How did you hear . . .?' gasped Daniel. Then he remembered the strange figure at the window on Halloween night. 'You're –'

Mr Hawthorne gave a nod.

Ten minutes later, the old Lupine and the young one were inside the house, sitting at Mr Hawthorne's kitchen table, drinking hot cocoa.

'You seem like a good kid, Daniel,' Mr Hawthorne said. 'Those other so-called Beasts can get a little carried away. You didn't belong with them. I had a feeling you weren't one of their kind.'

'I don't really know *what* kind I am,' said Daniel sadly, 'or where I "belong". I mean, the other boys love being wolves. My dad thinks it's the greatest thing ever, and I think even my twin brother is a little jealous he didn't get the gene. I don't understand why I'm not into it.'

'I do,' said the old man, sipping his cocoa. 'You see, I was never into it, either.'

Daniel stared at him. 'You weren't?'

'I was never much of an athlete when I was young. I was always happier to sit quietly with a good book, or write short stories and funny poems.'

Daniel smiled. *So Mr Hawthorne was kind of like me.*

'I fought it for years,' Mr Hawthorne explained. 'I read every historical tome I could find about werewolves, trying to discover a way to "reverse the curse", as I called it. But after a while I realised that this is who I am. So instead of going out with the other wolves and having fun, I always tried to use my super strength and vision and hearing to help people.'

'Like a superhero?'

Mr Hawthorne laughed. 'Not quite. A terrifying

werewolf can't exactly swoop in to save the day. But I found other ways of using my power for good. For example: once, in a coffee shop, I heard an old lady telling the waitress that her little dog was lost. That pooch was this poor soul's only companion and she was heartsick about it. So that night, I turned wolf and sent out a summoning howl.' He grinned. 'Just like your pal did the other night.'

'And the dog came back?'

'He was waiting on the old lady's porch the next morning.'

'So is this why you always close up your house on Halloween?' Daniel said. 'Because you're afraid your wolf form will scare the little kids.'

Mr Hawthorne gave a sigh. 'I know folks around here think I'm just a grumpy old man, but to my mind, that's better than giving some child nightmares.'

'Can't older wolves control the change?' Daniel asked. He knew his dad did not 'turn' unless he wanted to. Daniel was looking forward to the day he would be old enough to be 'in charge'. *I might just stay in human form for the rest of my life*, he thought.

Mr Hawthorne nodded. 'We can,' he said, 'but you'll learn that it's not a good idea to always keep the wolf inside. Even for me.'

The two werewolves sipped their hot drinks, enjoying a friendly silence. Then Daniel thanked Mr Hawthorne for the cocoa and said he had better get going.

'There's one more thing I should tell you,' said the older wolf as he walked Daniel to the door. 'It took me years to understand it, but once I did, it was one of the best discoveries of my life.'

'What's that?' asked Daniel.

'Well, as you know, our wolf selves are highly

tuned in to the world around us. That's why we see and hear so well. This *magic*, as I like to think of it, has a way of heightening all of our senses and abilities. Including our creative talents. I do my best writing when I'm in wolf form.' He picked up a hardcover book from the hall table and showed it Daniel. 'This is my latest publication,' he said proudly.

It was a children's picture book about a baby wolf that gets lost in the forest, but eventually finds his way home. Daniel had to laugh when he saw the author's name on the cover: Written and Illustrated by Lou Pyne.

'Thanks for the advice, sir,' said Daniel, shaking the old wolf's hand respectfully.

He pulled up his sweatshirt hood and bounded out into the night, filled with a new sense of hope. He'd never tried songwriting while in wolf form, but if Mr Hawthorne's theory was correct, maybe this whole Lupine thing could be useful to a budding rock star after all.

Maybe I won't *stay just in human form for the rest of my life.*

Justin poked his head into Daniel's room and yawned. It was almost two o'clock in the morning and Daniel was still hard at work, strumming his acoustic guitar and jotting down musical notes.

'What's going on?'

Daniel, who was still mostly in wolf form, looked up from his instrument. 'I'm writing a song,' he said. 'Well, actually, I'm *re*-writing a song.'

Justin frowned. 'Isn't it hard to play that thing with those claws?'

'Nope,' said Daniel. 'In fact, I'm really making progress. Turns out, being a werewolf doesn't just make you a better athlete. It can get your creativity flowing, too.'

'Cool.' Justin rubbed his eyes and flopped down on the foot of the bed. He was happy that Daniel had found something about being a wolf that he enjoyed. He doubted his brother would ever be truly OK with morphing into a hairy beast with fangs, but at least this was a start.

'Hope I didn't wake you up,' Daniel said, plucking out a few more notes, then scribbling them into his notebook.

'Nah. I couldn't sleep.'

Daniel put down his guitar. 'Weren't you able to work things out with Riley?'

Since he had already been in bed when Daniel had gotten home from wherever he'd been, Justin hadn't had a chance to tell his twin all about his amazing conversation with Riley.

And the kiss! Don't forget the kiss!

So Justin told Daniel all about how Riley was totally cool with everything. She'd sworn to keep the Packer family secret, and she didn't hold anything against Justin for being less than honest about it before now. Justin was about to reveal that he and Riley had shared their first kiss on the porch in the moonlight but at the last second, he decided not to. Daniel was still hurting over the Debi-situation, and hearing about Justin's romantic moment might make him feel worse.

'That all sounds great,' said Daniel. 'So why the insomnia?'

'Because after I left Riley's, I ran into Hunter and Devlin. Their super wolf ears heard *everything.*'

Daniel looked suddenly panicked. 'And? Were they mad that you told Riley?'

'Yeah,' Justin sighed, 'but they were mostly upset about the fact that we pulled a switch on them.'

Daniel sat up. 'They don't want you kicked off the team, do they?'

'I don't know yet,' Justin grumbled, throwing himself on to the floor and pulling Daniel's beanbag over his face. 'Tomorrow after practice, I have to meet up with them.'

Daniel put his guitar down. 'What for?'

Justin shrugged, and the beans in the bag rustled around him.

'Want me to go instead of you?' asked Daniel. 'Tell them I'm you and we lied to Riley for some reason. We can make up a reason why. The Beasts aren't that smart and I'm sure –'

Justin wrestled himself out from under the beanbag. He'd been thinking a lot about this and he'd made up his mind. 'No thanks, Bro. We've lied for long enough. I'm going with . . .' he gulped. 'The Truth.'

Justin hoped that truth would set him free. Just like Daniel said Elvis said it would.

Chapter Nine

Daniel glanced down the corridor to where Debi stood at her locker. She looked adorable as always, which made the idea of approaching her even scarier somehow. All he could seem to do was look . . . while trying to look like he wasn't looking.

Unfortunately, she must have sensed him staring because she suddenly glanced his way.

To avoid being caught, he quickly turned his head.

Clonk!

Even a werewolf boy felt pain when he

accidentally head-butted an open locker door.

He heard a little burst of giggles and sniggers, and somebody whispered, 'What a klutz!'

But he barely registered the insult. All he could think about was talking to Debi.

'Just be honest with her.'

Daniel jumped at the sound of Justin's voice in his ear. This got a few more laughs from the nosey onlookers and Daniel gritted his teeth. He was seriously going to have to tell his brother to lay off the long-range communication before it gave Daniel a heart attack.

Daniel shot a look to the opposite end of the corridor and found Justin giving him an encouraging smile. He motioned with his chin towards Debi, as if telling him: *Go for it, Bro.*

Daniel knew Justin was right. He took a deep breath and headed down the hall.

But just as he was about to reach Debi,

Mackenzie Barton appeared beside her. She was wielding her smartphone.

'Check this out!' she cried, handing the phone to Debi. 'It's an entertainment news video report – from where you used to live!'

Daniel's wolf hearing was able to pick up the video interviewer's voice clearly:

'We're here with up-and-coming young starlet Olivia Abbott in her charming home town of Franklin Grove,' said the interviewer. 'You may also know Olivia as the real girlfriend of teen heartthrob, Jackson Caulfield. And both of them are in Franklin Grove for a very special occasion.'

The interviewer went on to ask the girl called Olivia about the 'special occasion', which turned out to be the grand opening of a workshop for local artists called Café Creative. Olivia explained that the café was based in a long-disused wing of the Franklin Grove Museum and she said that she sincerely hoped this new venue would attract more creative youngsters to their small town.

Debi giggled. 'Same old Olivia. Always doing something cool.'

'Wait!' breathed Mackenzie. 'You actually *know* Olivia Abbott?'

'Sure. We went to the same middle school. I know her twin sister, too. They're an interesting pair.' She darted a look at Daniel. 'Total opposites.'

Daniel's heart thudded in his chest.

'OMG,' Mackenzie sneered. 'Olivia totally lucked out when she got that part in *The Groves*. I have it on DVD. Jackson was amazing as always, but she was a total amateur. And her hair was a dis-as-*ter*. I know it's all over the fan magazines that they're the new 'it' couple, but if you ask me, it's just a publicity stunt. I bet, in real life, Jackson probably can't stand her!'

Debi shrugged. 'I don't pay much attention

to the tabloids, but word back in Franklin Grove was that they fell for each other during filming.'

'And she gets to co-star in his next film, *Eternal Sunset*,' Mackenzie spat, snatching her phone back from Debi and frowning at Olivia's pretty face on the screen. 'Too bad they didn't film *The Groves* here in Pine Wood instead of Frankenstein Grove.'

'Uh, that's *Franklin* Grove.'

'Whatever. The point is, if Jackson Caulfield had come *here* looking for a leading lady, it *so* would have been me, and now I'd be the other half of America's hottest teen romance.'

Daniel let out a snort. He didn't know much about movie stars but he was pretty sure that, after five minutes in Mackenzie's company, this Jackson Caulfield dude would have hopped on the first plane back to Hollywood.

Mackenzie gave him a snippy look. 'What do you want, Daniel Packer?'

'A moment alone, actually.'

Mackenzie gave a long sigh. 'Fine. Debi, I'll see you in a few. Daniel wants to talk to me about something.'

'Not *you*!' Daniel rolled his eyes. '*Debi!*'

'Oh.' A faint blush coloured Mackenzie's cheeks, and Daniel was glad that she'd been put in her place. She was way too stuck on herself.

When Mackenzie flounced away, Daniel gave Debi a tentative smile.

She responded with an annoyed look.

'*How long are you going to stand there like a statue?*' Justin asked from the other end of the hall. '*Say something!*'

But Daniel continued to stand there like a statue, saying nothing.

'Homeroom is going to start soon,' Debi

prompted. 'I really want to hear what you have to say, but I don't want to be late.'

'Right. OK,' he blurted out eventually. 'Well, the thing is, I just want to say that I know I may have been acting a little weird lately.'

Debi gave him a half smile. 'Gee, ya think?'

'And I wanted to tell you, I'm sorry.' Debi seemed to be waiting for more, so he added, 'Um . . . *really* sorry.'

She looked up at him with her big blue eyes, and shrugged. 'I accept your apology.' Daniel was not as relieved as he thought he would be to hear that. Maybe because, even though the words were right, the body language was all wrong. She still looked upset. Maybe even a little hurt.

Daniel turned up his palms helplessly. 'I wish I could explain, but I can't.'

'You can't? Or you won't?'

'Both, I guess,' he answered honestly. 'But

you've got to believe me, I have a really good reason.'

'OK.' Debi turned away to take a book out of her locker. 'Forget it, then. It's really no big deal.'

There's that phrase again.

Daniel was beginning to understand that whenever Debi said something wasn't a big deal, she really meant that it *was* a big deal. It was as though Debi was self-conscious about letting him know how she really felt about things.

Boy, does that sound familiar!

From the scowl on her face, Daniel not explaining himself now was apparently a *very* big deal. He bit back a wolfish growl of frustration. 'Is there any way we can put all this behind us?' he asked, sounding almost as desperate as he felt. 'Can we go back to being good friends?'

Debi shrugged. 'I guess. But the Daniel I was friends with was honest, and wasn't afraid to be

191

his true self. I'm happy to be friends with *that* Daniel . . . if he's still around.'

With that, she turned and marched off to her Homeroom class.

Daniel watched her go, feeling like he hadn't solved anything. For all he knew, he'd made it worse.

Again, his thoughts were interrupted by Justin's voice. But this time, Justin wasn't talking to him – he was talking to Kyle and the other Beasts at the far end of the corridor. Something about their meeting after school. Justin was grumbling that he hadn't forgotten; he'd be there.

But he did not sound like he was looking forward to it.

As the Beasts swaggered down the hall, Daniel realised how ominous they looked when they were all together – like a true wolf pack. What were they going to do to Justin?

Daniel was about to approach his twin to offer his help again, when Riley appeared from around the corner, heading straight for Justin. When she took his hand and dragged him into the nearest empty classroom, Daniel decided this might be worth hearing.

He made his way down the hall and stood outside the door. Riley had closed it, but that wasn't a problem for someone with super wolf hearing.

'What was all that about?' she asked in a worried voice.

Daniel heard Justin sigh. 'Just football stuff.'

'So why do you seem so . . .?'

'Because I think they're going to throw me off the team,' said Justin.

It must be tough having the dormant werewolf gene, Daniel thought. *Poor Justin.*

'Well, at least there's an upside,' said Riley brightly.

'What's that?'

'If you get kicked off the team, you'll never have to hear Mackenzie cheer that silly chant she made up for you again.' Then she cried: *'Here comes Justin, Bustin' through the line! Packer the Attacker . . . scoring every time!'*

Daniel listened as Justin and Riley laughed together. He couldn't help himself. He was feeling jealous again. Why couldn't his relationship with Debi be this easy; this uncomplicated? Every time he tried to talk to her, he messed up.

In that moment, something occurred to him. Something a little bit crazy, but possibly crazy-brilliant.

Maybe *talking* wasn't the answer.

Chapter Ten

When Coach Johnston blew the whistle signalling the end of practice, Justin's heart slammed against his ribs. The entire Offense team were heading his way. When they reached him, Caleb put an arm around Justin and began leading him away.

This is it. I'm getting thrown off the team. I can feel it.

'We going somewhere, guys?' Justin gulped, hoping the fear didn't show in his voice.

'The woods,' Kyle answered curtly.

The Beasts guided Justin off the school grounds, towards the dense wilderness on the edge of town, where the werewolves had their super-secret Lupine gatherings. For the past two years, his father had told him about all the fun he would have, and the camaraderie he would experience at these werewolf get-togethers in the forest. Then he'd finally gone to one – unfortunately, he'd had to attend disguised as his brother, who was actually disguised as Justin. Just trying to work out the way they'd tried to cover up things over the last few weeks was enough to give Justin a serious migraine.

He wondered if it was *still* considered camaraderie if you were being *dragged* into the forest.

Maybe the second Caleb let go of him, he could make a run for it.

Yeah, right. Try running away from five werewolf jocks and see where that gets you.

Finally, they reached a large clearing, a wide treeless space where the ground was covered with tall grass and weeds.

Justin could see a burnt patch in the centre of the grass where many pleasant werewolf campfires had been held; where he had seen the Beasts howling into the night. Something Justin could never be a part of.

'OK,' said Kyle as Caleb and Chris sat Justin down on a rock. 'The way I see it, Packer, you've committed a pretty major crime.'

'I know,' said Justin. 'I should have never told Riley about the werewolves in Pine Wood, but I didn't have a choice. She saw Daniel turn into a wolf. How else could I explain it?'

Kyle was shaking his head. 'That wasn't the crime I was talking about.'

'It wasn't?'

'Nope. You *shouldn't* have told Riley about us, but she's a cool girl, and I'm sure she won't rat us out.'

'Oh.' Justin was so relieved he actually smiled. Then he remembered, 'So what *is* my crime, then?'

'You lied to *us*, dude!' said Ed. Justin was surprised to see that the big lug looked genuinely hurt.

'I'm sorry,' said Justin. 'I didn't mean to threaten our friendship.'

'Who's talking about friendship?' Kyle huffed. 'You threatened our team's *undefeated record*! You let us think you were one of us so you could make the offensive squad.'

'Yeah,' said Caleb. 'But you don't have super wolf speed, or agility.'

Justin felt a twinge of defensiveness. 'But I'm a good player. Better than most humans. And I think I've proven myself so far.'

'So far,' said Kyle, nodding.

Justin didn't like the sound of the quarterback's voice.

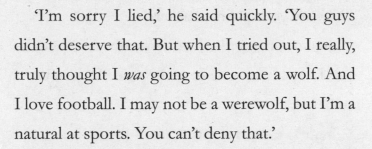

'I'm sorry I lied,' he said quickly. 'You guys didn't deserve that. But when I tried out, I really, truly thought I *was* going to become a wolf. And I love football. I may not be a werewolf, but I'm a natural at sports. You can't deny that.'

'The season's young,' Kyle explained. 'You've been able to hold your own until now. But what happens when the going gets tough? What happens when it's the last twelve seconds of the championship game and we're playing a team with some real skill? Will we be able to count on you, Packer? Will you play ball like you're a wolf, even though you're *not*?'

Before Justin could respond, Caleb picked up a football from behind another large rock. 'We like to keep these handy,' he said. 'We come out here to cut loose when we don't want the humans to see what we're *really* capable of.'

'Wait,' Kyle interrupted Caleb suddenly.

199

'Why are you smiling, Packer?'

Justin shrugged. 'Just remembering practice for Homecoming Game,' he said. 'A practice I survived.'

Kyle's eyes narrowed, and Justin knew the quarterback was remembering the intense drills they had run in the woods. Justin had run hard and fast, and he *knew* that none of the wolves had suspected a thing. He wasn't going to be able to fool them today, but he *was* going to show them that he could hang with them on the field.

'Drills,' barked Kyle suddenly. 'Let's see what you've got now.'

The Beasts formed their offensive line, with Justin in his usual position as running back. Kyle barked out the numbers and Ed hiked the ball.

Justin took off at full speed. It was eerie, running through a shadowy field of tall grass with no opponents gunning for him. It was kind of like playing against a team of ghosts – which, in Pine Wood, was not *that* weird an idea.

But he kept his focus and ran up the left flank. He knew Kyle could either throw the ball to Caleb, the wide receiver, who was moving like a blur up the right half of the clearing, or he could throw it to Justin.

Of course, since this was Justin's test, the ball came screaming in his direction. The pass was faster, harder and more furious than any Kyle would ever throw in a real game.

Justin leapt into the air and reached for it. It was like catching a cannonball! But he didn't let that stop him. He caught it and held it close to his body as he rolled in the long grass. He had made the play!

'Nice grab, Human,' said Chris, offering a knuckle bump as Justin got to his feet.

'Thanks, Wolf,' Justin replied with a grin.

Kyle called them back to the line of scrimmage and again called out the play – one in which he would hand off the ball to Justin.

Justin took the ball, thinking: *Great. Don't even have to catch. All I have to do is run – and there aren't even any opponents here to try and stop me. This will be too* easy.

But in the next second he realised how wrong he was.

The Beasts all turned to face him, re-assembling themselves into a defensive line. And what an impressive defensive line it was.

Justin felt his stomach flip. He'd rather attempt to run through the Great Wall of China – it would probably hurt less.

Chris came at him fast, stopping his charge and slamming him to the ground.

Justin's lungs felt as though they were on the verge of collapsing; he remained flat on his back in the grass, but managed to raise the ball into the air. 'Didn't fumble!' he grunted.

'Didn't gain any yardage, either,' growled Kyle.

With a groan, Justin got to his feet. 'OK,' he said, gasping for breath. 'Let's run it again, then.'

Kyle's eyes widened in amazement. 'You want to run the same play?'

'Yeah. Now. Let's go.' Justin was panting harder than ever, but he was ready.

'But Jordan just cleaned your clock.'

'I'm still standing, aren't I?' Justin tossed Kyle the ball. 'Let's do it.'

Once again, Kyle handed off to Justin, as the offense became the defense. Justin ran head-first into the wall of wolves. This time, Justin was prepared. He bent his head and aimed for the gap between them.

They weren't expecting the move, which worked in Justin's favour. His head and shoulders slipped through the slim space between Chris and Ed.

But these guys weren't amateurs. When they saw what he'd done, they immediately tightened around him.

It's like being caught in a gigantic vice.

Justin still didn't quit. He hadn't hit the ground, so the ball was still in play. He gritted his teeth and pumped his legs with every ounce of human strength he had. It was like running through quicksand, but he didn't give up. He pushed harder, faster . . .

Yes! He actually managed to drive them back!

One yard . . .

Two . . .

He barrelled forwards, feeling like he was pushing a dump truck up a hill. The Beasts were snorting and grunting. Justin was giving them a run for their money, but they weren't about to back down any more than he was.

'Whoa!' Justin cried, as the sky seemed to fall down in front of his face. He felt weightless as his legs and head swapped places –

Whommmmmpppffff!

As his back collided with the earth, the echoing thud seemed to rattle the whole forest. Justin knew that this was the sound of his football future coming to an end.

Justin closed his eyes and let it sink in. *I'm finished. Thirteen years. Football is done. And all for a few dumb yards!*

The Beasts were milling around, murmuring, and he hated the sound of it; he knew they were probably trying to decide who was going to have the honour of telling him he was out. Justin was hauling himself back up – every bone aching – when, again, Kyle appeared over him. He offered Justin a hand and helped him to his feet.

'You fell short, cubby,' Kyle said in a sombre voice. 'If this were a real game, we'd be in danger of losing possession.'

Justin bowed his head. He knew what was coming. Kyle was going to tell him he didn't have what it took to play for the Pine Wood Wolves. He was going to throw him off the team. He was going to . . .

Offer me a high five?

Justin blinked. Kyle had raised his palm and was waiting for Justin to smack it.

'I don't understand,' said Justin. 'You just said —'

'I know,' said Kyle, a grin spreading across his face. 'If you ever played against a whole pack of werewolves you might not make your yardage every single time. But c'mon, there's never going to be a real game where we go up against guys *half* as strong as us. You just proved that you can hold your own against *werewolves*. You're human, but you're fast. And you're strong. And most important, you've got courage. You didn't give up.'

Justin needed a second to digest this. His entire body hurt – he couldn't begin to imagine the amount of bruises he'd have in the morning. When he was finally able to process what Kyle had said, he smiled. 'I'm still on the team?'

'Absolutely. You're a talented football player, for a guy without fangs.'

Justin laughed. 'Thanks.'

'It was never personal,' Kyle clarified. 'We just wanted to make sure you wouldn't be bringing us down. And now we know you won't.'

Justin was giddy. He'd worked things out with Riley *and* he was going to get to stay on the team. *This is shaping up to be an awesome day*, he thought, accepting the painful high fives and fist bumps his teammates offered.

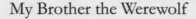

Then he heard his cell phone chirp.

He'd completely forgotten it was in his pocket, and with the way the Beasts had been tossing him around for the last half hour, he was surprised to find that it hadn't shattered into a million pieces.

It was a text message from Daniel – short, to the point, and a little bit troubling:

I NEED YOUR HELP

'Gotta go, guys,' said Justin.

'But, dude,' Kyle looked confused, 'you're on the team. What could be more important than that?'

Justin didn't answer. He took off, running at top speed, dodging low branches and hurdling fallen logs. Despite all his bruises and sore muscles and exhaustion, he ran and ran and ran.

Daniel wanted his help. Nothing could slow Justin down. Football meant the world to him, but his twin brother meant the universe.

Chapter Eleven

'I can't believe I ran all the way home for *this*!' Justin grumbled, eyeing himself in Daniel's bedroom mirror.

'Well, you did,' said Daniel, 'and I appreciate it.' He adjusted the collar of the leather jacket Justin was wearing. It was Daniel's jacket. Justin was also wearing Daniel's snug fitting black T-shirt and his tattered blue jeans. 'You look great.'

He remembered just a little while ago hassling his brother for spending too much time obsessing over his appearance, but now Daniel was the one wanting perfection. Especially now, when having the perfect look would be crucial. And when so much would be riding on it.

Of course, at the moment, Justin's look was actually Daniel's look. Justin had been transformed from a clean-cut jock to the lead guitarist of a gnarly rock band.

'It's freaky,' said Daniel, handing Justin his old guitar. 'You totally could pass for me.'

'Oh, really? And what was your first clue? When the doctor wrapped us in blankets and said, "They're twins"?'

Daniel laughed, giving his brother a nudge towards the door. 'You know the plan, right?'

'Yeah,' sighed Justin, striding down the hall. 'We're going to Debi's house, where I'm going to stand outside her window. You're going to hide behind a tree and play the new guitar and I'm going to pretend to play this cruddy old one, while lip-syncing the song you wrote for her.'

211

Daniel winced when Justin said his two most-hated words in the English language – *lip-syncing*. But in an emergency like this, what choice did he have? 'The song I *re*-wrote for her,' Daniel clarified. 'It's way better now.'

'It's a good idea,' said Justin, as the boys headed down the stairs. 'I'd even go so far as to say it's "romantic". But I still think *you* should be the one standing under her window. Haven't we learned the hard way that switching places usually brings us nothing but trouble?'

Daniel sighed. 'Believe me, there's nothing I'd rather do more. But look.' He jerked up his sleeve, revealing an arm covered with fur. 'Between my nerves and what's left of the full moon, I'm already half wolf-i-fied. I'd rather take my chances with one more switch than risk turning right there on Debi's lawn.'

'I see your point,' said Justin as they reached

the front door. 'But can I have the cool guitar instead?'

Daniel pulled open the door. 'No.'

'Boys?'

The twins froze at the sound of their mother's voice, keeping their backs to her for fear that she'd know they were up to something the minute she saw their faces.

'Where are you off to?' she asked.

'Just going outside to see how my guitar sounds in the night air,' said Daniel, then cringed. *Stupid.*

'Interesting,' said Mom. 'Well, good luck with that.'

The boys had just stepped out the door when Mom called, 'And by the way, Justin, you look great in Daniel's jacket!'

They could hear her chuckling softly as the door closed.

'She's good,' Daniel said, shaking his head slowly.

'Yeah,' agreed Justin. 'I guess it's a mom thing.'

On the way to Debi's, Daniel made Justin recite the new-and-improved lyrics, which Justin had somehow managed to memorise in five minutes. He made a few small goofs, but for the most part, he knew them cold.

'If you forget any of the words, just duck your head and pretend you're *really* concentrating on your playing. That way she won't be able to see your lips *and* it'll look totally intense.'

'OK. As long as you don't break into some hard-core improv riff I won't be able to fake, we should be fine.'

'I won't,' said Daniel. 'This means way too much for me to wing it. There will be no noodling from me tonight.'

Justin squinted at him. 'What's this got to do with noodles?'

'Never mind,' said Daniel.

He was on his way to win Debi round to thinking he wasn't the most terrible guy in the world. Everything had to go perfectly.

Two boys, two guitars and one amplifier set out across the street.

The amp was attached to an extra-long extension cord which Daniel had plugged into the outside electrical socket under their front porch, hidden behind his mother's azaleas.

When they arrived at Debi's house, Daniel ducked behind a large oak tree while Justin took his place beneath Debi's second-storey window. Between the glow of the moon and the lamppost on the sidewalk, there was just enough light so that Justin was visible. And so were all the pumpkins, ghosts and crazy Halloween decorations. The place looked like more of a graveyard than a front yard. Debi's dad really was into Halloween.

Daniel hoped the hanging skeleton wasn't a bad omen. 'OK,' he whispered, arranging his fingers on the guitar strings. 'One . . . two . . .'

'Wait!' Justin hurried over to the tree. 'I can't go through with this!'

Daniel almost dropped his guitar. 'Justin, you promised.'

'But you know I'm a lousy singer.'

'You're not singing, you're . . .' Daniel coughed before uttering the words, '*lip syncing*, remember?'

'Oh, right.' Justin frowned, eyeing the cool jacket he was wearing. 'But it's still a bad idea.'

Daniel flung his arms wide. 'You said it was a *good* idea!'

'The part about you serenading Debi with an original love song is a great idea. The part about me *pretending* to be you serenading Debi with an original love song,' Justin shrugged '. . . not so much.'

'But you *have* to!' growled Daniel, tugging up his sleeve. 'If I do it, I'll wolf out.'

Justin grinned. 'You sure about that?'

Daniel looked down at his arm. No fur! His arm was completely normal. He was about to serenade Debi with a song he wrote straight from his heart and he wasn't even nervous!

'I don't get it,' said Daniel.

'Maybe it's like when I was proving myself to the Beasts this afternoon,' Justin offered. 'When you're doing something that really matters to you, you can kind of rise above the nerves. You just do it because it comes naturally to you and you forget everything you're scared of.'

'Maybe you're right,' said Daniel. 'And I'm pretty sure if I hide behind this stupid tree instead of singing to Debi, I'll *definitely* regret it.'

'Well, then,' said Justin, clapping his brother on the back, 'what are you waiting for?'

Daniel took a deep breath, ran a hand through his hair and stepped out into the little pool of light cast by the lamppost.

Just as he was about to play, a car zoomed down their street, thumping over the fat extension cord.

Daniel's eyes flew open.

'It's OK,' Justin assured him in a whisper. 'That cord is industrial strength.'

Daniel let out a sigh of relief and let his fingers touched the strings. *This is who I am – the real me. I have nothing to be nervous about.*

He strummed the first chord, expecting the music to fill the yard and bring Debi rushing joyfully to her window.

But the only sound the guitar made was a faint

metallic *twang*, a tinny whisper.

'Did you remember to plug it in?' Justin whispered.

'Yes,' Daniel whispered back. 'The car must have yanked the plug out of the socket.'

Both boys let their eyes follow the orange electrical cord that ran from the back of the amp, over the Morgan's spook-filled front lawn and across the street to the Packer's porch.

Apparently, extra-long wasn't long enough!

The plug had come out of the socket and was visible in the grass in front of the azaleas, falling a good three feet short of the electrical source.

'It doesn't reach,' sighed Daniel. 'Now I can't play the song. I might as well just give up.'

'No!' said Justin. 'Listen, Bro, tonight I played a game of one-on-five tackle football with a bunch of guys who eat raw meat for breakfast, and I didn't quit! So that means you're not going to quit, either. You should just sing it.' He knit his brows in thought. 'What's it called when you sing a song without musical accompaniment? "Rocka-fella?"'

Despite his nerves, Daniel laughed. '*A cappella*,' he corrected.

'Whatever – it's romantic. Do it.'

Daniel nodded. 'You're right. But first I have to get Debi's attention.' He bent down, picked up a pebble from the ground and cocked his arm back, preparing to throw it.

'Are you nuts?' cried Justin, grabbing his wrist. 'With your wolf strength you'll shatter the whole window.' He grinned and took the little stone. 'This is one thing I *will* do in your place.'

Justin aimed, lobbed the pebble and ran; he was back crouched behind the tree before it hit the glass with a gentle *clack*.

They waited.

A lifetime. Or maybe five seconds. To Daniel, it felt like an eternity.

'Maybe she's a heavy sleeper,' said Justin.

'Maybe she's calling the cops,' said Daniel.

In the next moment, a light bloomed in the window and Daniel's heart nearly stopped. Then the sash went up and Debi's confused face was peering down at him.

'Daniel?' she whispered, leaning over the sill. 'What are you doing?'

In reply, Daniel began to sing.

> *'Moonlight Girl, I'm in a midnight whirl,*
> *You smile and the stars forget to shine,*
> *Your blue eyes are a brilliant surprise,*
> *Someday I'll make you mine . . .'*

He sang just loudly enough for Debi to hear, but he put everything he had into it. The revised melody was even prettier than before and the words were more imaginative and heartfelt. His wolf senses really *had* made him a more talented songwriter!

'Hair like fire, you're my one desire,
I dream about you every night.
Moonlight kissing is what I'm missing,
You're the one who'll make it all right.'

Daniel was so into the serenade that he actually closed his eyes to sing the last verse.

'Now I'm wishing on stars and searching the sky,
Hoping that I'll be your only guy.
You shine like moonbeams from above,
Moonlight Girl, can this be love?'

He held the final note just long enough so that it didn't become a howl.

I did it. And I did it great! Now she'll definitely know how I feel. Smiling, Daniel opened his eyes and lifted his gaze to Debi's window.

But Debi wasn't there.

Daniel stared at the empty window, his whole body feeling empty. His silent guitar suddenly seemed to weigh a ton.

She didn't listen. She didn't stay.

Justin was beside him now, placing a brotherly hand on his shoulder. 'Tough break, man. Sorry.'

Then Daniel heard the creak of the front door opening.

'That's probably Mr Morgan coming to throw me off his property,' Daniel gasped. 'Run!'

Justin took off like a shot but Daniel's foot caught on something – the extension cord – and he went down hard, making a perfect face plant in the Morgan's front yard.

Is this cord cursed?

Daniel was about to launch himself back on to his feet when a pair of fluffy pink slippers appeared beside his head.

He didn't think they were Mr Morgan's.

He looked up from the slippers and into a smiling face. It was the girl with hair like fire. The Moonlight Girl herself, live and in person.

'Debi?'

She smiled at him. It was the brightest smile he'd ever seen. *Moonbeams. Definitely.*

'Hi,' said Debi.

'Hi.'

For a moment they just stared at each other awkwardly.

'Um . . . do you need a hand getting up?'

Daniel was so flustered that he'd actually forgotten he was lying face down in the grass.

He scrambled to his feet.

'That's better,' he muttered.

Debi giggled, her eyes sparkling. 'Great song.'

'D'you think so?'

She nodded. 'It may be my favourite song in the whole world.'

Daniel grinned. 'Mine, too.'

'Only problem is, I left the window before I heard the last verse.' She bit her lip and tilted her head and Daniel's knees nearly gave out. 'Would you sing it again, please?'

'Sure,' said Daniel; he would sing it for her as many times as she was willing to hear it. He'd sing it *a cappella*, and he'd sing it with his band. He'd even sing it for her with a full concert orchestra backing him up, if he could get his hands on one.

They were friends again, and that thought filled him with happiness.

'*Pssst.*'

Daniel turned to see Justin across the street, grinning at him. When his brother pointed to the

225

electrical cord, Daniel understood that Justin had managed to plug in the amp by adding another extension cord.

He gave Justin a thumbs-up, then turned back to Debi, who was now sitting on the grass with her knees drawn up and her chin resting on them.

She was ready to listen.

And he was ready to sing.

Ready to tell her how he felt. No switching, no fibbing, no chickening out.

He arranged his fingers on the guitar strings and then the music began, filling the yard, the street and the moonlit sky as Daniel sang from his heart.

He sang to the Moonlight Girl.

Repartee With Riley – October Edition!

Hello, Pine Wood pupils! A special treat for you today. I'm sure you're all HUGE fans of our very own destined-to-be-rock-stars *IN SHEEP'S CLOTHING*, and are eager to have a better understanding of how a song is written. So, our guitarist and songwriter Daniel Packer has – after MUCH persuasion – allowed me to publish a 'Before and After' of his latest masterpiece! It's a cute love ballad that is SURE to have all you couples dancing at the upcoming Valentine's Day ball. Yes, I know there isn't actually a Valentine's ball booked at our school, but Mr Grant, you just KNOW I'm going to make it happen!

Moonlight Girl

(Final Version)

Lyrics by Daniel Packer. Music by In Sheep's Clothing

A smile as bright as stars.
Hair that shines like fire.
Like a puppet I am yours,
You got me dangling on a wire.

CHORUS:
Moonlight Girl, I'm in a midnight whirl,
You smile and the stars forget to shine,
Your blue eyes are a brilliant surprise,
Someday I'll make you mine.

Thundering weather, until we're together,
Stormy clouds, unless you're around.
Only when we're alone do I feel at home,
Moonlight Girl, don't leave me all alone.

CHORUS

Hair like fire, you're my one desire,
I dream about you every night.
Moonlight kissing is what I'm missing,
You're the one who'll make it all right.

CHORUS

Now I'm wishing on stars and searching the sky,
Hoping that I'll be your only guy.
You shine like moonbeams from above,
Moonlight Girl, can this be love?

Moonlight Girl

(First draft)

Lyrics by Daniel Packer. Music by In Sheep's Clothing

A smile as bright as stars.

(Start song with lights low)

Hair that shines like fire

(Now lights fade up slowly)

Like a ~~puppy~~ puppet I am yours

(too close to the bone!)

You got me dangling on a wire

Moonlight Girl, ~~I'd love to see you do a twirl~~

I'm in a midnight whirl,

(Maybe do a whirl here, to make the point)

You smile and ~~I almost wolf out~~

(True... but not romantic)

the stars forget to shine,

Your blue eyes are a brilliant surprise,

(check they are definitely blue, and not contacts)
Someday I'll make you mine.

Terrible weather, until we are together
(need a more terrible word than terrible)
Stormy clouds, unless you're around
Only when we're alone do I feel at home
(would this be a good place to jump off
the stage and pick her out from the crowd?
Not sure there will be time between
lines, though!)
Moonlight Girl, don't leave me all alone.
(Heartfelt howwwwwwl, Nathan to harmonise.)

Hair like flames, stop playing silly games
Hair like fire, you're my one desire,
I dream about you every night.
(Not every night. Sometimes I dream about
wolfing out in public. And not revising for tests.
Suitable material for a different song?)

Moonlight kissing is what I'm missing,
~~I think of you when I'm running through the night~~
You're the one who'll make it all right.

Now I'm wishing on stars and searching the sky,
Hoping that I'll be your only guy.
You shine like moonbeams from above,
Moonlight Girl, can this be love?

(If she freaks out, change lyrics to:
Moonlight Girl, you know it's true.
I really, totally, quite like you.)

COMMENTS ON THIS FEATURE:

MACKENZIE says: Some of the words have been scribbled out so hard that I can't read them! What do they say?

DANIEL PACKER says: A songwriter's got to have some secrets!